Alice Maude Kellogg

Christmas Entertainment

Alice Maude Kellogg

Christmas Entertainment

ISBN/EAN: 9783337379728

Printed in Europe, USA, Canada, Australia, Japan

Cover: Foto ©Andreas Hilbeck / pixelio.de

More available books at **www.hansebooks.com**

CHRISTMAS ENTERTAINMENT

BY

ALICE M. KELLOGG

NEW SONGS TO OLD TUNES
FANCY DRILLS
ACROSTICS
MOTION SONGS
TABLEAUX
SHORT PLAYS
RECITATIONS IN COSTUME

NEW YORK AND CHICAGO
E. L. KELLOGG & CO.

CONTENTS.

PAGE

NEW SONGS TO OLD TUNES :
Time for Santa Claus........M. Nora Boylan......... 7
Santa Claus is Coming......Maud L. Betts........... 7
Old Santa Claus.............M. Nora Boylan......... 8

FANCY DRILLS :
A Christmas-bell Drill.......Ella M. Powers.......... 9
The Snow Brigade..........Marian Loder............ 10
Christmas Stockings.........A. S. Webber............ 11

ACROSTICS :
Christmas Children.........M. Nora Boylan......... 13
Santa Claus.................W. S. C................. 14
Charity.....................Jay Bee................. 15
Merry Christmas............M. D. Sterling........... 15

MOTION SONGS :
A Christmas Lullaby.................................. 18
Dance of the Snowflakes......Alice E. Allen........... 19
Little Snowflakes............Ella M. Powers.......... 22
Christmas Stories...........Lettie Sterling.......... 23

TABLEAUX :
Christmas Pictures.................................. 24

RECITATIONS IN COSTUME :
The Brownie Men............M. Nora Boylan......... 27
Winter's Children...........J. D. Moore............. 27
Santa Claus.................Julia C R. Dorr......... 29
Father Christmas' Message..J. A. Atkinson.......... 31

SHORT PLAYS :
Mr. St. Nicholas............Alice M. Kellogg........ 31
Christmas Offerings by Chil-
   dren from Other Lands.....Ella M. Powers.......... 37
A Christmas Reunion........M. D. Sterling 41
Christmas Waits............Katherine West 49
A Christmas Party..........Lizzie M. Hadley........ 51

3

PAGE

RECITATIONS FOR THE PRIMARY GRADE:

Santa's Helpers..............M. Nora Boylan......... 58
Christmas Eve..............Eugene Field............ 59
Santa Claus' Visit...........Susie M. Best 59
To Santa Claus..............Jennie D. Moore......... 60
What I Should Like.........Jennie D. Moore......... 61
A Gentle Reminder..........Alice W. Rollins........ 61
Christmas Time.............M. N. B................. 62
Christmas Wishes...........C. Phillips.............. 62
Christmas Morn.............M. N. B................. 63
My Christmas Secrets........S. C. Peabody........... 63
Kriss Kringle...............Susie M. Best........... 64
A Message ....Ella M. Powers.......... 65
The Mousie.................M. N. B................. 65
A Letter from Santa Claus...William Howard......... 66
The Christmas We Like......Ella M. Powers.......... 67
Saint Nick..................M. N. B................. 67
Merry, Merry Christmas.....Carine L. Rose.......... 68
Christmas Questions... .....Wolstan Dixey 69
A Catastrophe..............Susie M. Best........... 69

RECITATIONS FOR THE GRAMMAR GRADE:

A Christmas Gift...........Mabel L. Pray........... 70
A Christmas Thought ......Lucy Larcom............ 72
The Merry Christmas Eve ...Charles Kingsley 73
The Christmas Stocking..... Charles H. Pearson...... 73
Christmas Hymn............Eugene Field 75
Bells Across the Snow.......F. R. Havergal 76
Christmas Eve..............Frank E. Brown......... 77
The Little Christmas Tree....Susan Coolidge.......... 78
The Russian Santa Claus ....Lizzie M. Hadley........ 80
A Christmas Garden.................................. 81
A Christmas Carol..........J. R. Lowell............. 82
The Power of Christmas. 83
Peace on Earth......... ....S. T. Coleridge.......... 84
The Christmas Tree 85
Old English Christmases............................. 86
Holly and Ivy ....Eugene Field........... 87

NOTE.

A LARGE proportion of the material in this collection was contributed to *The School Journal.* It is distinguished from other selections by the author's name following directly after the title.

Permission to use copyrighted poems has been kindly given by the publishers of *The Outlook*, New York City; *The Ladies' Home Journal*, Philadelphia; *Good Housekeeping*, Springfield, Mass.; Mrs. Alice W. Rollins, Bronxville, N. Y.; Houghton, Mifflin & Co. and Roberts Brothers of Boston; and Charles Scribner's Sons, New York.

Christmas Entertainment.

❦

Time for Santa Claus.

By M. NORA BOYLAN.

(To be sung to the tune of " Ta-ra-ra, boom-de-ay.")

Now's the time for Santa Claus ;
Christmas comes with loud huzzas.
Hark ! the bells ! Oh, hear them ring !
Ting-a-ling-ling ting-a-ling.

Cho.—Ting-a-ling-ling ting-a-ling,
　　　Ting-a-ling-ling ting-a-ling,
　　　Ting-a-ling-ling ting-a-ling,
　　　Ting-a-ling-ling ting-a-ling.

See his prancing reindeer brave,
Hear him tell them to behave—
Dasher, Dancer, Prancer, Vixen,
Comet, Cupid, Donder, Blitzen.—*Chorus.*

Yes, hurrah for Santa Claus !
Blow the trumpets, shout huzzas !
We'll be happy while we sing—
Ting-a-ling-ling ting-a-ling.—*Chorus.*

❦

Santa Claus is Coming.

By MAUD L. BETTS.

(To be sung to the tune of " Marching thro' Georgia.")

Santa Claus is coming—we shall welcome him with glee:
He'll hang a gift for every one upon the Christmas-tree ;

He'll not forget a single child.   How happy we shall be;
         For Santa Claus is coming.

Chorus—

Hurrah ! hurrah ! for Christmas time is near ;
Hurrah ! hurrah ! the time to all so dear ;
We all shall hang our stockings up when Christmas eve is
    here,
         For Santa Claus is coming.

But we must remember all that we must do our part ;
Christmas is the time of times, to give with all our heart.
We must always share our joys with those who have no
    part,
         When Santa Claus is coming.

Old Santa Claus.

By M. NORA BOYLAN.

(To be sung to the tune of "Yankee Doodle."   The verses may be
given by a single voice, with the chorus by the school, or selected voices
on the platform.)

    Old Santa Claus is a jolly man
      Who brings us lots of toys, sir ;
    And none are happier Christmas time
      Than little girls and boys, sir.

    Have you not seen our Santa Claus,
      With hair so snowy white, sir ?
    Just hang your stocking Christmas eve,—
      He'll come that very night, sir.

    And if you watch, perhaps you'll see
      This friend in furs hid deep, sir.
    But I have never seen him once—
      I'm always fast asleep, sir.

Chorus—Santa Claus is jolly, sir ;
        Santa Claus is kind, sir ;
        Santa Claus on Christmas eve
          Comes riding on the wind, sir.

A Christmas-bell Drill.

By ELLA M. POWERS.

(This drill may be given by eight little girls provided with wands. At the top of each wand are tacked three streamers of red, white, and blue ribbon or cambric. At the end of each streamer a little tinkling bell is sewed. The children sing, and wave wands in time to the music. The words may be sung to the tune of " Lightly Row.")

Sweetly chime, sweetly chime,
Happy bells of Christmas time ;
Sweetly chime, sweetly chime,
　Christ the Lord is born.

Christ is born, our Saviour dear,
Joyous words we love to hear ;
Sweetly chime, sweetly chime,
　Christ the Lord is born.

(Between first and second verses, all march singing same tune to " Tra la la."—" Tra la la," wands waving, up, down, right, left, up, down, right, left, throughout. Resume places and sing second verse.)

Sweetly chime, sweetly chime,
Happy bells of Christmas time ;
Sweetly chime, sweetly chime,
　Glory be to God.

Let us carol sweetly then,
Peace on earth, good will to men ;
Sweetly chime, sweetly chime,
　Christ the Lord is born.

(All march out, singing. and waving wands.)

The Snow Brigade.

By MARIAN LODER.

(*A winter drill for a dozen boys—in overcoats, earcaps, bright-colored mufflers, mittens, etc. Each carries a big snow-shovel. The stage should be spread with sheets and loose cotton to represent snow. Boys come marching in single file, shovels over shoulder, singing to the tune, "See the Farmer in the Field."*)

I.

We are the jolly Snow Brigade,
With our trusty shovels we make a raid,
And lustily we'll give you aid
On a frosty winter's morning.

Chorus.—He ! he ! ha ! ha ! ha !
He ! he ! ha ! ha ! ha !
He ! he ! ha ! ha ! ha !
Ho ! ho ! ho !

II.

(*Beginning to shovel cotton.*)
We'll shovel your walk for fifteen cents,
We'll pile the snow against the fence,
We'll show you we are boys of sense
On a frosty winter's morning.—*Cho.*

III.

(*Rubbing noses.*)
Jiminy crack ! our noses are cold !
Oh ! Jack Frost is bad and bold !
(*Working harder than ever.*)
But little care we for the winter cold,
On a clear and frosty morning.—*Cho.*

IV.

(*Pointing to work.*)
Look at that ; now what do you say ?

(*Holding out hands to audience.*)
>Now, if you please, we'll take our pay.
>Our work is done, it's time for play,
>On a frosty winter's morning.—*Cho.*

(*Begin snowballing with the cotton, throwing balls into audience and at each other.*)

Christmas Stockings.

By A. S. WEBBER.

(Six small girls and boys are needed for speaking, and any even number of larger girls for singing. A boy leads each division of the march, immediately followed by those who speak.

An equal number enter from opposite sides as far back as possible, pass in front to sides, back half-way, form two lines across front, having the six who speak in front (alternating boy and girl), and the larger pupils back of them sing as they enter and until they are placed the chorus of " Birdies' Ball," beginning " Tra la la la la." When in position all sing the following two verses, air, " Birdies' Ball." When chorus is reached, let them keep time by resting weight on right foot on first count, and at same time swinging left foot over right, touch toe to floor, dipping body slightly on third count, foot back in place on first count of next measure. Rest weight on left foot and swing right foot over left, touching right toe on third count, foot back in place on first count of next measure, etc.)

>Santa Claus on Christmas eve,
>>Means to give a gift to all,
>Each a stocking we will hang,
>>Stockings big and stockings small.

Chorus.—Tra la la la, etc.

>Santa Claus on Christmas eve
>>Comes with reindeer swift as air,
>Early all must be in bed,
>>Leaving only stockings there.

Chorus.—Tra la la la, etc.

(A girl comes one step forward, bows, and speaks.)

>I mean to hang on Christmas eve
>>A stocking of this size (*measures*),
>Because I want a doll so big,
>>That sleeps and shuts its eyes.

To crowd it in a stocking small
Would surely not be wise.

(Pupil steps back in place and all sing the chorus, keeping time as before.)

2d Pupil.— My stocking is the one I'll hang,
I know 'twill hold quite well,
About a hundred marbles more
Than's owned by Tommy Bell.
Of course I want some candy, too,
But the marbles are what tell.

(Steps back, and chorus is repeated as before.)

3d Pupil.— I mean to beg a stocking small
Of little sister Clare,
Because I want some things so small
They'll scarce be found e'en there.
I want a ring that has a stone,
And a pretty pin to wear.

(Chorus repeated as before.)

4th Pupil.— I've measured all the stockings round,
And think I'll hang up two,
Because I want a pair of skates,—
One stocking will not do.
Of course I want some sweets and things
To last the whole week through.

Chorus, etc.

5th Pupil.— My mamma's stocking I will hang,
'Twill so much better hold
A tea-set for my dolly dear,
All painted round with gold ;
And dishes can't be squeezed, you know,
That's what I've oft been told.

Chorus, etc.

6th Pupil.— And I don't know just what to do,
Because I want, you see,
A hobby-horse that is so high,—
Now tell me, can it be,
Are stockings ever made so big
That one can hold all of me ?

Chorus, etc.

All sing.— All we children love to hang
   Stockings o'er the fireplace,
    Wondering how our gifts can come
   Nice and clean from such a place.

Chorus. — Tra la la la, etc.

    Santa Claus is loved by all
    Folks who are as big as we,
    And for long before he comes
    We can only sing for glee.

Chorus. — Tra la la la, etc

(When the chorus is partly sung, the leaders of the march lead to opposite sides, others fall in line forward, pass in front to rear along sides, pass
at rear end to seats.   Continue to repeat the chorus till all are seated.)

Christmas Children.

By M. NORA BOYLAN.

(An acrostic for the primary grade.   Each child wears a large gilt star
around his neck.   As he begins to speak, he turns it over, showing his letter on the reverse side.)

  All : Happy children here we stand.
    Bringing words of love ;
    For on this glad Christmas day
    Christ came from above.

 First child : C is for the Christ Who came
    To this lowly earth.
Second child : H is for the harps that rang
    At our Saviour's birth.
 Third child : R is for the ringing bells,
    Telling Christmas-tide.
Fourth child : I is for the crystal ice
    Where we go to slide.
 Fifth child : S is for the schoolboy's sled
    When he coasting goes.
 Sixth child : T is for poor Tommy Jones—
    Jack Frost bit his nose.

Seventh child : M is for the merry part
                 Of this Christmas day,
Eighth child : A is for the apple pies
                 Grandma put away.
Ninth child : S is for old Santa Claus,
                 Coming here to-night.
                 Hope he'll wait till nearly morn,
                 So it will be light.

All : Yes, we're happy children nine,
           And to each we're true,
           Three cheers for jolly Santa Claus,
           A happy day to you.

Santa Claus.

By W. S. C.

(A letter exercise for ten very small children. Let each child present a placard bearing the letter as he recites his line. At the close, all shut their eyes and screw them up very tight.)

S stands for stockings we hang up so high.
A is for all we get if we don't cry.
N is for nobody he will pass by.
T is for to-morrow, the day we eat pie.
A stands for at last old Santa is nigh.

C for the children who love him so well.
L for the little girl, his name she can spell.
A stands for apples so rosy and red.
U is for us as we wait for his sled.
S stands for Santa Claus, who comes in the night
    when we are tucked up in bed with our eyes
    closed so tight.

Charity.

By JAY BEE.

(Seven little girls daintily dressed carry a bell in the right hand, with the initial on it which begins her line. The bells are rung lightly during the speaking)

First child : Cheerily ring the Christmas bells !
Second child : How joyfully their jingling tells
Third child : All peace and kindness on the earth,
Fourth child : Ringing out, singing out, laughing with
mirth !
Fifth child : In every home is joy profound,
Sixth child : The echo of this merry sound.
Seventh child: Yet Charity must remembered be,
And that is why we have this tree.

Merry Christmas.

By M. D. STERLING.

(Seven boys and seven girls with good voices and some sprightliness of manner are required. Each carries a wand, to the upper end of which is fastened an evergreen wreath surrounding a large, gilt letter. Ranged in order the letters will spell the word "Merry Christmas." The verse for each is sung to the air, "Buy a Broom." The children enter only one at a time, using a polka step, boys and girls alternately. While singing they take steps and wave wand in time to music. At third line of each stanza the boys bow and the girls make a courtesy, right and left. The chorus at the end of each verse is sung by the entire school. The boy with letter M comes in first, sings, and takes position on platform. He is followed by the girl with E. So continue until the line of children is complete.)

First boy :

M stands for merry—oh ! let us be merry ;
M stands for merry—right merry am I.
(*Bowing.*) With a bow to the right, sir, and a bow to the
left, sir,
Come, now, and be merry, all sadness defy.

Chorus (*by school, to the refrain of " Buy a Broom"*).—

Christmas dear now draws near,
With song and with evergreen welcome it here.

First girl :
E stands for evergreen, beautiful evergreen,
    E stands for evergreen, never to fade.
(*Courtesying*.) With a courtesy to right, sir, and a court-
    esy to left, sir,
    Bring evergreen garlands for Christmas time made.
                                                    —*Cho.*

Second boy :
R stands for rollicking—come, then, be rollicking ;
    R stands for rollicking—fun's in the air !
With a bow to the right, sir, and a bow to the left, sir,
    In Christmas-day rollicking take now a share.—*Cho.*

Second girl :
R stands for rally, a grand Christmas rally,
    R stands for rally, where Christmas trees grow !
With a courtesy to right, sir, and a courtesy to left, sir,
    We rally where Santa is likely to go.—*Cho.*

Third boy :
Y stands for youthful—rejoice, now, all youthful ;
    Y stands for youthful—quite youthful am I.
With a bow to the right, sir, and a bow to the left, sir,
    The youthful make merry when Christmas is nigh.
                                                    —*Cho.*

(Leave a space in the line of children between the last letter of " Merry "
and the first of " Christmas.")

Third girl :
C stands for Christmas—bright Christmas, merry Christ-
    mas ;
    C stands for Christmas—the best of the year.
With a courtesy to right, sir, and a courtesy to left, sir,
    Make merry at Christmas with good Christmas cheer.
                                                    —*Cho.*

Fourth boy :
H stands for happy—at Christmas be happy !
    H stands for happy—right happy am I.
With a bow to the right sir, and a bow to the left. sir,
    If you would be happy some Christmas gifts buy
                                                    —*Cho.*

Fourth girl:
R stands for ready—for Christmas be ready ;
  R stands for ready—are *you* ready yet ?
With a courtesy to right, sir, and a courtesy to left, sir.
  To make ready for Christmas, oh ! never forget.—*Cho.*

Fifth boy:
I stands for icy—for winter so icy ;
  I stands for icy, when Kris drives along.
With a bow to the right, sir, and a bow to the left, sir,
  Though icy the weather we'll give him a song.—*Cho.*

Fifth girl :
S stands for Santa—the children's own Santa ;
  S stands for Santa, the jolly old dear.
With a courtesy to right, sir, and a courtesy to left, sir,
  For Santy to fill we hang stockings each year.—*Cho.*

Sixth boy :
T stands for thoughtful—of all friends be thoughtful ;
  T stands for thoughtful—your presents prepare.
With a bow to the right, sir, and a bow to the left, sir,
  And be thoughtful those poorer than you have a
    share.   —*Cho.*

Sixth girl :
M stands for magic—for Christmas-night magic ;
  M stands for magic filling stockings and tree.
With a courtesy to right, sir, and a courtesy to left, sir,
  Who does this fine magic, can any agree ?—*Cho.*

Seventh boy :
A stands for all of us, old and young, all of us ;
  A stands for all of us looking for Kris.
With a bow to the right, sir, and a bow to the left, sir.
  And all of us hope that not one will he miss.
                                              —*Cho.*

Seventh girl :
S stands for smiling—on Christmas morn smiling ;
  S stands for smiling—all smiling I'll be.
With a courtesy to right, sir, and a courtesy to left, sir,
  All smiling, yes, smiling, when presents I see.—*Cho.*

(The following verses are to be sung by the school to the air, "Wait for the Wagon." During the singing of the first stanza and chorus, the fourteen boys and girls divide off into couples and march around, elevating and lowering the wands in time to music. During the second stanza they form two opposite lines, with wands crosseo overhead, couples marching under the arches formed and back again to places. Third stanza, the opposite lines pass forward and back, cross to other side, partners passing each other, then back once more, and turn partners into place in a line forming "Merry Christmas" again.)

Oh, Christmas, merry Christmas!
Thy call we must obey,
And carry fadeless garlands
In honor of the day.

Chorus (to be sung after each verse).—
All hail, merry Christmas!
Hail, merry Christmas!
All hail, merry Christmas,
The evergreen day.

Oh, Christmas, merry Christmas!
With laughter, song, and play,
How gayly pass the hours
Of that dear, happy day.—*Chorus.*

Oh, Christmas, merry Christmas!
Quite old, but never gray,
Like thy own joys, unfading,
The wreath we bring to-day.—*Chorus.*

A Christmas Lullaby.

(The children are seated in little rocking-chairs, each holding a doll dressed in a long white gown. They rock slowly in time to the music. At first 1 "hushaby" they raise forefinger of right hand, as if to insure silence.
2. Kiss dolls.
3. Very softly.
4. Lay dolls in small cradles, standing near.
5. At "hush" raise forefinger of right hand warningly.
6. Very softly.
7. Rock cradles slowly in time to music, children kneeling on floor.
8. Turn toward audience.
9. Very softly.
The words are adapted to the music of the familiar hymn, "Silent Night.")

Hushaby, hushaby, (1)
Christmas stars are in the sky ;
Sweet the bells of Christmas eve,—
Babies, each a kiss receive,— (2)
Hushaby, good-night,
Hushaby, good-night ! (3)

Lullaby, lullaby,
Babies in their cradles lie ; (4)
Every one in white is gowned,
Hush, make not a single sound ! (5)
Lullaby, good-night,
Lullaby, good-night ! (6)

Rockaby, rockaby,
Christmas-tide draweth nigh ; (7)
Quiet now the tiny feet,
Babies sleep so still and sweet,—
Sweetest dreams, good-night, (8)
Sweetest dreams, good-night ! (9)

Dance of the Snowflakes.

By ALICE E. ALLEN.

(The words of this motion song are adapted to the chorus of " Dream Faces." The children should be dressed in white gowns, white stockings and slippers, and wear caps made of white tissue paper, trimmed with silver stars.

1. Raise both hands, look up.
2. Move hand slowly back and forth, with floating motion.
3. Lower hands, and motion as if swaying cradle.
4. Drop head slowly to one side, close eyes as if sleeping.
5. While pianist plays last half of song slowly, children take hold of corners of skirts, and with waltz step dance from side to side, still with sleepy look and motion.
6. Stand erect, with eyes wide open.
7. Use forefinger of right hand as if enforcing command.
8. Raise both hands above head, and lower them slowly, with fluttering motion.
9. Drop heads, sing very slowly.
10. Shake heads sadly.
11. Look down as if searching for flowers.
12. While pianist plays as in 5 children repeat 5 very slowly, still look ing down.

13 Music much faster and brighter.   Children look up over right shoul
der, as if afraid of being caught.
14 Whir round and round.
15 Bend to right, and then to left.
16. Fall lightly to floor.
17. Spring up with hands upraised.
18. Drop hands, smile.
19 All clasp hands, raise them high above heads, and dance lightly
backward and forward
20. Hold position 19; dance as in 5, only more rapidly.
21. Dejected position, heads bent down.   Music very slow and sad.
22. Raise and lower right hand slowly.
23. Repeat with left.
24. Music strong and faster.   Children raise on tip-toe of right foot,
reach forward with motion as looking in window above them on their
right.
25 Motion with forefinger of right hand as if counting stockings.
26 With skirts distended dance as in 20, smiling.
27. Right hand raised to ear, as if listening.
28. Shade eyes with right hand and look expectant.
29. Step forward, both hands extended as if in greeting, smiling.
30. Throw kiss to audience.
31 Pianist repeats all of song ; children dance as in 26, singing verse
beginning " Bright stars are gleaming," and at last " Merry Christmas "
throw kiss to audience.)

We lived in cloudland, (1)
Floating here and there (2)

Over the mountains
And the valleys fair.
Winds swayed our cradles, (3)
Then we fell asleep, (4)
While far above us
Stars their watch did keep. (5)

" Wake," cried the North Wind, (6)
" You to earth must go." (7)
Down we fell fluttering (8)
Butterflies of snow.
Silently and slowly (9)
Through the winter hours,
Falling so sadly, (10)
Hiding grass and flowers. (11–12)

Then the wind caught us, (13)
Whirled us round and round, (14)
Dashed us and drove us, (15)
Piled us on the ground (16)

Flying up in frolic, (17)
Always glad and gay, (18)
Dancing and drifting (19)
All the stormy day. (20)

Now our play is over, (21)
Now the day is done,
Falling so sadly, (22)
Sadly one by one. (23)
Peeping in the windows (24)
Where the fires glow,
See the children's stockings (25)
Hanging in a row. (26)

Hark, in the distance (27)
Hear the merry bells !
Santa Claus is coming, (28)
Sweet their music tells !
Go we now to greet him, (29)
Listen as we call,—
Glad merry Christmas,
Merry Christmas all ! (30)

Bright stars are gleaming, (31)
Christmas cometh soon.
Joy bells are ringing,
All in merry tune.
We are Christmas snowflakes,
Singing as we fall,—
Glad, merry Christmas,
Merry Christmas all !

Little Snowflakes.

By Ella M. Powers.

(Six primary children may sing these words to the tune, "Tiny Little Snowflakes" in "Golden Robin," with the following finger-play.

a. Hands waving up and down, fingers moving rapidly

b. Imitate the waving with hands and heads to right and left.

c. Quickly shake head and hands.

d. One sweep of hand across the desk.

e. Right hand raised as high as head, fist closed.

f. Abruptly bring fist down on desk.

g. Similar to (*a*).

h. Hands clasped and eyes upturned as if gazing with admiration at the tree.)

We are little snowflakes, (*a*)
　　Falling gently down,
On the fields and mountains
　　In the busy town.

Now the waving (*b*) spruce trees
　　Shaking (*c*) gently say,
Brush away this light snow, (*d*)
　　It's nearly Christmas day.

Then a man comes gayly
　　With his axe so bright, (*e*)
He chops down the spruce tree (*f*)
　　Early one fair night.

Then on Christmas morning
　　Children dance to see, (*g*)
Many lovely presents
　　On that stately tree. (*h*)

Christmas Stories.

By LETTIE STERLING.

(These stories may be said and done in concert, or each little child may give one verse by himself.

a Hands held straight up so tips of fingers point toward ceiling.

b. Touch palm of hand with thumb, bring it back quickly.

c, d, e, f. Repeat *b* with 1st, 2d, 3d, and 4th fingers.

g. Double the hand up.

h. Place the doubled-up hand on the back of the other.

i. Lift thumb and hold it up.

j. Lift 1st finger.

k. Lift 2d finger.

l. Lift 3d finger.

m. Lift 4th finger.

n. Hold hands in a listless way, with tips of fingers pointing toward floor for two first lines, and let the fingers gently swing. Near the close of the verse make the fingers still and rigid and hold them close together.

o. Have hands doubled up and held so that the child's eyes can look down upon the palm of the hand and see the nails of the four fingers—thumb out of sight.

p. Let fingers fly up quickly

q. Hold left hand as in *a*. Use the index finger of the right hand as a match, scratching it on the palm of the left hand and lighting the tips of each finger as if the fingers were candles.

r. Make a circle of a thumb and index finger of the right hand and slip it on and off each finger on the left hand.

s. Bunch fingers of left hand together so they can all touch the tips of the thumb and form an opening for the window.

t. Bring the fingers of the right hand near and let them be boys and girls peeping in.

u. Double up hands, but instead of having thumb inside, let it stand straight up to be a tower.

v. Snap the fingers of one hand, then of the other.

w. Point far away with index finger.

x. Point toward an imaginary star.

y. Hold up the three middle fingers.)

Chimneys standing in a row, (*a*)
Down each one will Santa go.
He goes down one, comes back alive, (*b*)
And then tries two, (*c*) three, (*d*) four, (*e*) and five. (*f*)

Santa has a wondrous pack, (*g*)
This he carries on his back ; (*h*)
From it he takes candies, (*i*) drums, (*j*)
Dolls, (*k*) books, (*l*) trumpets, (*m*) when he comes.

Near the chimney stockings swing,
What to them will Santa bring ?
All of them I'm sure he'll fill,
Make them round and stiff and still. (*n*)

Morning kisses curly heads
Lying snugly in their beds, (*o*)
O how quickly they hop out, (*p*)
Seizing stockings with a shout !

On the hemlock and the pine,
Light the candles, make them shine ; (*q*)
String the rows of corn so white (*r*)
'Mong the gifts and tinsels bright.

Storemen's windows all look gay,
'Cause it's near to Christmas day. (*s*)
Come and look in, girls and boys, (*t*)
Get a peep at Christmas joys.

In high towers out of sight
Great bells ring with all their might ; (*u*)
Hear one, then another chime, (*v*)
Telling it is Christmas time.

In the distance, look afar, (*w*)
With their eyes upon the star, (*x*)
Come on camels wise men three, (*y*)
They the Christmas King shall see.

Christmas Pictures.

(This set of pictures is suggested by Mrs. Kate Douglas Wiggin's story of "The Birds' Christmas Carol," published by Houghton, Mifflin & Company, Boston, Mass. Each picture should be preceded by descriptions from the book ; these are indicated by the number of the page in the volume.

DIRECTIONS.—A good reader must be chosen, who can bring out the light and shade in the story—one who can make the listeners feel the pathos of Carol's brief, helpful existence and the contrasting homely humor of "the Ruggleses in the rear." A reading-desk and lamp must stand below the platform, and the audience-room be left in darkness. The reader will give the signal for the opening and closing of the curtains, pausing long enough for a full recognition of the scene. As a repetition of a tableau is often more successful than its initial effort, the performers should be on the alert, prepared to give a second view.

The characters in the story call for six young people to represent Mr. Bird, Mrs. Bird, the Grandmother, Physician, Mrs. Ruggles, and Uncle Jack, and fourteen children to take the parts of Donald, Hugh, Paul, Carol, Sarah Maud, Peoria, Cornelius, Eily, Kitty, Peter, Clem, Larry, Susan, and the boy singer.

The first hymn, " Carol, Brothers, Carol," is to be sung behind the cur-tains, just before they are drawn for the second picture. A harp, violin, and triangle would assist the piano in making an orchestral effect. A solo voice supplies the closing air, " My Ain Countree." The piano may be played very softly whenever the reader pauses and the tableaux are shown.

It is important that the arrangements for each scene be made in absolute quietness, with systematic forethought, else the attention of the listeners will be distracted from the reading.

If a Christmas tree for the entire school is to close the entertainment, it should be in readiness at the rear of the platform, concealed by a cur-tain. In the sixth picture the tree appears, to illustrate the story, and remains lighted through the evening.)

FIRST PICTURE.

" They were consulting about it in the nursery." (Page 1 in " The Birds' Christmas Carol.")

In this scene the children's belongings are scat-tered about: small chairs, a cradle, toys, and pic-ture-books. Mr. Bird stands in the center of the platform holding a large doll dressed in infant's robes. Grandma is seated near, and Uncle Jack, Donald, Paul, and Hugh are discussing a name for the baby. The Christmas hymn is heard after the curtains are drawn and before the

SECOND PICTURE.

" A famous physician had visited them." (Page 12.)

Mr. and Mrs. Bird and the doctor are seated around a library-table in earnest conference.

THIRD PICTURE.

Carol's " Circulating Library." (Page 16.)

Carol is lying in an easy-chair beside a case filled with books. The description of her room should be carried out on the stage as far as practicable.

FOURTH PICTURE.

" The children took their places." (Page 36.)

The nine Ruggles children are seated in a row

facing the audience. Mrs. Ruggles stands before them, giving instructions about their behavior at Carol's dinner party. The costumes must be fantastic, following the description in the story—green glass breastpin, the purple necktie, and much-braided hair.

FIFTH PICTURE.

" The feast being over," etc. (Page 35.)
Carol's room is shown again. The Ruggles children are seated around Carol, with Mr. Bird and Mrs. Bird and Uncle Jack in the background.

SIXTH PICTURE.

"There stood the brilliantly lighted tree." (Page 55.)
The same characters that appeared in the preced·· ing scene are shown in attitudes of delight and astonishment as the second curtain is drawn aside to show the Christmas tree.

SEVENTH PICTURE.

" Softly, Uncle Jack." (Page 63.)
The library is shown again. Mr. and Mrs. Bird, Uncle Jack, Donald, Hugh, and Paul are grouped as if listening attentively. At the right of the plat·· form a leaded-window effect is made with a slender wood frame covered with black gauze. Behind this stands a small boy in choir vestments, holding a music book and singing " My Ain Countree" to organ accompaniment.

The Brownie Men.

By M. Nora Boylan.

(An exercise for four little boys. They wear padded trousers of some cheap brown material and a loose shirt of same material in place of the school jacket. Skull-caps of same material, worn jauntily. Broad white rings about the eyes and charcoal lines upon face to produce resemblance to pictured Brownies. Jolly smiles and capers. Join hands and hop on one foot around tree or 'eader, before, between, and after verses.)

Merry, merry sprites are we,
Dancing round the Christmas tree.
We've a gift for every one
Though the last one is just done.

This has been a busy year,
And we hope we bring you cheer,
And when Christmas comes again,
Look for us—The Brownie men.

Winter's Children.

By J. D. Moore.

(The children should wear some indication of the several characters they impersonate. Most elaborate and beautiful costumes might be used, but the simple device of a placard upon each child's breast bearing the name of his part will answer the purpose.)

Wind : I come from the cold and stormy North,
With a rush and a roar I hurry forth,
I toss from the trees the dead leaves down,
The withered leaves all sere and brown,
And sway the branches to and fro
As on my way I whirling go.
At crack and crevice I slip in,
And make a lively sounding din.
Swift I come and swift away,
With you I can no longer stay,
For I am wanted elsewhere now,
And so good-bye, I make my bow,

Frost (*taking Wind's hand*) :

Hand in hand we ever go
Through the season to and fro.
I breathe upon the streams.   They cease
Their murmurings and are at peace.
Upon each window pane I trace
The finest filmy glistening lace.
Each boy and girl, 'tis plain to see,
Hath still a welcome kind for me.
For on the lake they whirl and wheel,
You hear the click of polished steel
As swift upon their skates they fly
With joyous heart and flashing eye.
My breath blows cold.   Health, joy, delight,
Follow my silvery sparkles bright.
Now Snow, who is my guardian sweet,
Will all my young friends fondly greet.

Snow (*a little girl*) :

Over the earth so bare and brown
I spread a robe as soft as down.
Drifting, drifting down through space,
Hiding each unsightly place,
Touched to shimmering radiance bright,
In the moonbeam's mellow light,
By my brother Frost, for we (*they join hands*)
Both go hand in hand, you see.
North Wind goes gaily with us both,
To help us he is nothing loath.
And he and Frost and Rain combine
To give what in the clear sunshine
Shimmers sparkling—pure and nice,
Transparent, white, and glistening Ice.

Ice : I cling to lofty gables, I rustle 'mid the snow,
I weave a gleaming covering
For lakes and streams.   They know
That all must cease their murmuring
When Frost and I appear,
For we will hold them firm and fast
As long as we are here.

Gleaming, glistening, sparkling,
Yet pure and clear and bright.
You'll find me 'neath a silver moon,
Each crisp, fresh winter night.
             (*Enter Old Winter.*)

Winter : What, ho ! my children, here I am,
         I've sought you everywhere.
         And now to busy work away,
         For you must all prepare
         To do your duty while I hold
         In check your enemy,
         The great round sun, whose rays with you,
         My children, disagree.
         Now up, away ! Wind, to the west
         And come again in glee ;
         And join with Frost and Snow and Ice,
         In one grand jubilee.
         And paint the cheeks with roses
         Of all these children who,
         Right joyously will run and shout,
         My children dear, with you.
         Away ! to work, you must not shirk
         Your duties, dears ; and now,
         To these, your firmest friends, make each
         Your most engaging bow.
(*All bow and retire Old Winter following.*)

Santa Claus.

(Let the first line be given by a small boy as a herald, carrying a
trumpet, and dressed in tunic, tights, and velvet cap. The second line is
taken up by Santa Claus, in costume of fur, with white beard and hair.)

A voice from out of the northern sky :
" On the wings of the limitless winds I fly,
  Swifter than thought, over mountain and vale,
  City and moorland, desert and dale !

From the north to the south, from the east to the west,
I hasten regardless of slumber or rest ;
O, nothing you dream of can fly as fast
As I on the wings of the windy blast !

" The wondering stars look out to see
Who he that flieth so fast may be,
And their bright eyes follow my earthward track
By the gleam of the jewels I bear in my pack.
For I have treasures for high and for low :
Rubies that burn like the sunset glow ;
Diamond rays for the crownèd queen ;
For the princess, pearls with their silver sheen.

" I enter the castle with noiseless feet—
The air is silent and soft and sweet ;
And I lavish my beautiful tokens there—
Fairings to make the fair more fair !
I enter the cottage of want and woe—
The candle is dim and the fire burns low ;
But the sleepers smile in a happy dream
As I scatter my gifts by the moon's pale beam.

" There's never a home so low, no doubt,
But I in my flight can find it out ;
Not a hut so hidden but I can see
The shadow cast by the lone roof-tree !
There's never a home so proud and high
That I am constrained to pass it by,
Nor a heart so happy it may not be
Happier still when blessed by me !

" What is my name ?　Ah, who can tell,
Though in every land 'tis a magic spell ?
Men call me that, and they call me this ;
Yet the different names are the same, I wis !
Gift-bearer to all the world am I,
Joy-giver, light-bringer, where'er I fly ;
But the name I bear in the courts above,
My truest and holiest name, is—LOVE ! "

JULIA C. R. DORR.

Father Christmas's Message.

(This speech may be given at the close of a Christmas entertainment.
A white wig and beard, fur coat and gloves are worn, and sleigh-bells are
sounded before Father Christmas appears on the platform.)

Here I am again. The close of the year
Brings Old Father Christmas with his good cheer.
I'm cheery myself, and cheery I make
All folks who follow advice for my sake.
My advice is the same to all my friends :
Give and forgive, and quickly make amends
For what you do wrong.   Let love be the rule.
Christians, be true at the season of Yule.
Old Father Christmas every one welcomes ;
I bring peace and happiness to all homes.
Away with the bad.   Have nothing but good.
Do what I tell you.   If only you would,
You'd all live at one in true brotherhood.
I always brighten up all hearts.   The spell
Of Christmas can all gloomy thoughts dispel.
My friends, right pleased am I to see you here.
How are you all ?   Pray come again next year.
I hope you've liked the fun we've had to-night ;
If so, then now applaud with all your might.

J. A. ATKINSON.

Mr. St. Nicholas.

By ALICE M. KELLOGG.

(The characters are Old-fashioned Santa Claus, dressed in the tradi-
tional costume of fur, white beard, and a Christmas pack ; Mr. St. Nicholas, in evening dress with silk hat ; Dora, Katie, Maggie, and little Bess ;
Harry, Charlie, Tom, and John in ordinary school clothes.
    The scene opens with a large fireplace arranged at the center of the plat-
form, a dark curtain drawn before the opening to conceal Santa Claus.
The accompaniment to " Nancy Lee " is heard, and the eight children
march in, carrying their stockings.)

Oh, Christmas time has come again,
    Tra la la la, tra la la la;
We welcome it with glad refrain,
    Tra la la la la la.

Of all the happy holidays this year
There's none so joyous, none so dear,
Then sing we all our song of festive glee,
Of Santa Claus and Christmas tree.

Chorus.—Oh, ring the bells, the merry Christmas bells,
          Their music all our pleasure tells.
(*Repeat, singing tra la la whenever necessary to give the rhythm. They pause in groups in center, right, and left; some sit, others stand, and change their positions during the dialogue*)

Harry: Oh dear, the same old thing again this year, I suppose ! " Hang up the baby's stocking, be sure you don't forget."

Charlie: This baby's stocking is the biggest bicycle hose I could buy. (*Pins it at one side of the chimney.*) I don't think old Santa could miss it if he tried.

Dora: I made mine to suit the occasion, for I hope Santa Claus will fit a zither into it. (*Displays a large, fantastically shaped stocking of striking color, and fastens it beside Charlie's.*)

Harry: You ought to take a prize, Dora, for designing the most—ahem!—unexpected-looking stocking. Generous sized, too ! Here goes my contribution to the chimney. (*Hangs up a sock.*) It's big enough to hold a coin of gold that will buy me a new bicycle. I don't care for any knick-knacks.

Katie: I must confess that I'm rather tired of this old custom of hanging up our stockings on Christmas eve and crawling out of bed in the cold dawn to see what is in them. I wish some one would invent a new way.

Maggie: Just what I thought, Katie, last winter, though I never spoke of it. But if you've hung your stocking up, I must have mine there too. (*Goes to chimney.*)

John: Well, I refuse to fall in line this year. I'm tired of the whole plan. It seems absurd for an old chap to come tumbling down the fireplace and load up our stockings.

Tom: I agree with you, John! What we want is a new-fashioned Christmas. A real, up-to-date Santa Claus, and no more of this children's nonsense.

Bess: Not have Santa Claus any more? Isn't he coming to-night? (*Cries.*)

John: Oh yes, he'll remember you if you're a good little girl and stop crying. Dora, help Bess to fasten up her stocking.

(*After the stocking is fixed, Bess faces the audience and recites.*)

Bess: I do hope dear old Santa
    Will come this way to-night,
And come here to my stocking,
    To fill it nice and tight.

I'd like to watch and see him,
    But I know I must wait
Till shines the Christmas sunshine—
    I hope he won't be late.

Tom: Let Bess have her old-fashioned Santa Claus, but the rest of us vote for something different.

Harry: I used to think Santa a pretty jolly old duffer, who made lots of sport for the infants, but I'm ready for a change myself.

Dora: Don't count me in to help out your majority; Santa Claus seems to me the kindly spirit of Christmas appearing mysteriously to give us greater pleasure.

Katie : Well, I'll side with the boys this time, and see if there is any improvement in holiday matters.

Charlie : You'll think me a baby to stick to the old style.   I won't venture an opinion at all.

Tom : Then we are agreed that of Santa Claus we have no need.

John :
Kate : } 'Tis what we all concede.
Harry :
Maggie:

(*All sing to the tune* of " *Maryland, My Maryland.*")

> Old Santa Claus is such a bore,
> Of him we've had too much and more ;
> Now what we want is something new,
> But what is there for us to do?
> A new St. Nick would be the thing,
> Who would our Christmas presents bring.

(*Electric bell sounds, the door opens, and Mr. St. Nicholas comes on the stage.   He bows and takes off his hat.*)

Mr. St. N.: Good evening, young people! I see you are at your old-time tricks of hanging up your stockings.   This won't do.   Don't you know it's gone out of fashion? (*Goes toward fireplace ; the boys rush to protect their property.*)

John : Who are you, sir? And how dare you interfere with our fun?

Mr. St. N.: I am the new, up-to-the-times Santa Claus.   My proper name is Mr. St. Nicholas. I am on my rounds to take the names of all the young people who deserve a remembrance at Christmas time.   I haven't a moment to lose.   My telephones are overburdened with messages, my men are distracted with the work to be done between now and daylight. (*Pulls out a book and pen-cil and prepares to write while he addresses Tom and speaks rapidly without waiting for a reply.*) Your name, young man? Your age, birthplace, parents' names? Residence? Attendant at what school? What specific tastes? List of last year's presents. Make haste, time is money.

Katie: But Santa—I mean Mr. St. Nicholas—here are our stockings.

Mr. St. N.: Christmas stockings! trash and non-sense. They belong to the dark ages.

Harry: Pray, how do you bestow your gifts?

Mr. St. N.: By district messenger service, of course! Next boy (*to Charlie*), give me your name, age, birthplace, parents' names, residence, school, specific tastes, last year's presents.

Charlie: How did you come here, Mr. St. Nich-olas? I heard no sleigh-bells at the door.

Mr. St. N. (*scornfully*) : More nonsense to ex-plain. I came down from the north pole in an air-ship of the latest pattern. Come, now, here are these girls waiting to be classified. (*To Dora.*) Name, age——

Dora: I won't be put in statistics, even if it is Christmas and you are the patron saint.

Charlie: Nor I. I didn't vote for any improve-ments. Take them away.

John: You seem a trifle ahead of the age, Mr. St. Nicholas, or else we made a great mistake in being discontented with our old-fashioned Christmas.

Tom: Allow me to call down your air-ship.

(*Mr. St. Nicholas is ushered to the door. The others turn back at the sound of sleigh-bells. Santa Claus appears at the fireplace.*)

Children (*greeting him with enthusiasm*) : Jolly old Saint Nicholas!

Santa Claus : Oh! ho! ha! ha! Are you really glad to see such an old-fashioned specimen as I am?

John : Indeed we are! We have just shown your usurper the door.

Bess (clasping S. C.'s hand) : You are the real Santa Claus.

Santa Claus : Yes, I am the real Santa Claus, and I cannot get to work until you children are fast asleep. So scurry away as fast as you can, and a merry, merry Christmas when you awake!

Children (singing to the tune of " Nancy Lee," and at the end leaving the stage):

> Oh! Christmas time has come again,
> > Tra la la la, tra la la la.
> We welcome it with glad refrain,
> > Tra la la la la la.
> Of all the happy holidays this year,
> There's none so joyous, none so dear,
> Then sing we all our song of festive glee,
> Of Santa Claus and Christmas tree.

Chorus.—O ring the bells, the merry Christmas bells,
> Their music all our pleasure tells. (*Repeat.*)

(*Santa Claus unpacks his goods, and as he fills the stockings he performs various antics, holds up the objects, and dances about. Any local expressions that will create amusement he can bring in with running commentaries. The piano is heard softly till he is through, and then bursts out loudly as the curtain is drawn.*)

Christmas Offerings by Children from Other Lands.

By ELLA M. POWERS.

(DIRECTIONS.—This exercise may be given by six little girls. The platform may be decorated with evergreen trees or boughs, and flags should be used freely. The American girl should be dressed in an American flag and wear a cap of red, white, and blue. The costumes of the others may be as follows :

The Eskimo girl should procure a boy's fur coat, or wrap a fur rug about her and wear a fur cap or hood and fur mittens.

The Indian girl can throw about her a gay-colored blanket, and wear strings of beads about her neck, arms, and head. Her straight dark hair should be parted in the middle, plaited in two braids in the back, and decorated with short pieces of bright ribbons. Moccasins and dark brown stockings may be worn on the feet. Bracelets, earrings, chains, beads, quills, and brooches may be used as ornaments. The hands, arms, and face should be stained. To color the skin get a stick of Hess Grease Paint No. 17. Rub a little vaseline into the skin to be tinted. Then rub a portion of the paint on the palm of the left hand and with the fingers of the right hand transfer it evenly to the skin surface until the required tint is obtained.

The Chinese girl should be dressed brightly with large, square, loose hanging sleeves, a broad sash tied on one side, her hair brushed flat, coiled in the back, with haircomb and pins thrust into the coil. She may have a Japanese parasol and carry a fan.

The African girl may be dressed in red and black, with black hair and red handkerchief over her head and large rings in her ears. Face and hands blackened with burnt cork.

The Arabian girl can wear a tunic or bright shawl draped about her, a turban of a bright silk handkerchief, and wear feathers in her hair. She should be very dark-complexioned.

. The American girl enters, takes her seat in the center of the platform, saying :)

American girl :

    And this again is Christmas day ;
      My invitations all
    Have gladly been accepted ;
    Let us see who first will call.

(Eskimo girl enters, bows, comes forward with a fur bag filled with presents, which she passes to the American girl as she mentions them.)

Eskimo girl :

    I'm a little Eskimo girl,
      I live in the land of ice,
    We never saw a Christmas tree
      Nor fruits and candies nice ;

But we run races o'er the snow,
    Beneath the big, bright moon,
And from this far away ice-land,
    I've brought you a nice bone spoon.
My father hunts all through the day
    For reindeer, seal, and bear,
And sends away in ships so strong
    These furs so rich and rare,
And fish, and birds, and whales, you know,
    I've seen them many a time,
And here's a pretty fur for you
    That came from the arctic clime.

(Eskimo girl offers presents and steps to one side. American girl bows
and places presents on the boughs beside her. Enter Indian girl.)

Indian girl :

I'm a little Indian girl,
    I live in the far Northwest,
In the land of the Dakotas,
    In the land I love the best.
I've brought a nice bead-basket,
    I made it all. You see

I know about your Christmas
    A happy day to thee.
And here's an arrow-head for you,
    And a piece of pottery queer,
And here are herbs for medicine good,
    To make you strong, my dear.

We children shoot and fish and hunt
    Just as our fathers do,
The whole wide forest is our home ;
    It feeds and clothes us, too.

(Steps aside. Enter Chinese girl.)

Chinese girl :

I'm a little Chinese girl,
    They say I've almond eyes,
I live in a boat, on a river we float,
    And often eat rice and rat pies.

And here is a bamboo basket,
Filled with choicest tea,
I picked and dried it all myself
It comes from Ken See Lee.   (*Bows low.*)

With us we have no Christmas,
No presents nor a tree ;
But there in the boat, I made this toy,
This, too, comes from Ken See Lee.

(Chinese girl bows low and takes a seat on low stool in front of Ameri
can girl.   Enter African girl.)

African girl :

I'm a dark little African girl,
I live in a forest land,
With kinky curls and jet black eyes,
I watch the elephant band.

My father hunts these animals,
From one of them I bring
An elephant's tusk to you, my friend,
'Twill make you a pretty ring.

And here is ebony wood for you,
A cocoanut from the palm,
And dates to eat, so very sweet,
All from our African farm.

(Offers presents, which American girl hangs on the boughs. African girl
steps to her left.   Enter Arabian girl.)

Arabian girl :

I'm a little Arabian girl,
I live in a desert land,
In tents on the plain so hot and dry,
And I play on the burning sand ;

Here is a pretty pearl I've brought,
And an ostrich's egg so rare ;
An Arab pony you should have
And a cloak of camel's hair.

I never hear about Christmas,
And don't-know what you mean,
But hope you will accept these gifts,
And this ostrich feather green.

(Offers gifts. American girl accepts them, rises, places them on tree; then turns and repeats :)

American girl :

And I'm a happy American girl,
How thankful I should be,
That Christmas is so bright a day
And means so much to me.

I thank you, friends, for all these gifts,
Of presents I've my share ;
And *you* show *your* good-will to men
With generous gifts so rare.

(All stand in line and repeat together :)

All : Our countries all are glorious lands,
So great, so rich, so rare ;
Our people all are glorious bands ;
So true, so good, so fair.

Whatever country we are from,
Whatever life we lead,
We'll do our best ; be good and true,
And do some noble deed.

A Christmas Reunion.

By M. D. STERLING.

CHARACTERS REPRESENTED: *Father Christmas*, a large boy dressed in long belted robe ; he carries a staff, and wears a white wig and beard. *Mother Goose*, a tall girl wearing a peaked soft hat tied over an old lady's frilled cap ; also neck-kerchief and apron ; spectacles on nose, and a broom of twigs, such as street-cleaners use, complete her costume. *Mother Goose's* son *Jack* and her *Children* may be costumed according to the pictures in any good illustrated copy of " Mother Goose." The *Children of the Nations* are sufficiently represented by boys and girls each carrying one of the flags of all nations, but elaborate costumes in keeping with the national character may be used, if desired. *Thanksgiving* and *Happy New Year*, large girls in white Grecian dresses, flowing sleeves ; their children, *Peace* and *Plenty*, *Good Resolutions* and *Hope* are represented by smaller girls in white, *Peace* carrying an olive branch, *Plenty* a cornucopia, *Good Resolutions* a diary and pen, and *Hope* wearing a wreath of golden stars and carrying a gilt anchor (cut from heavy cardboard) ; *Santa Claus*, a stout, roly-poly boy, if possible, wearing a long overcoat flaked with cotton (to represent snow) and a round fur cap and mittens ; an empty pack should hang carelessly from one shoulder.)

(Enter *Father Christmas* and *Mother Goose*, arm in arm. While conversing, they walk up and down the platform. At the end of Mother Goose's second speech, they seat themselves in two large arm-chairs, which should be ready in middle of platform.)

Mother Goose :

Well, well, Father Christmas, I'll do as you say,
And put off my trip for the frolic to-day.
Your thought of a Christmas reunion is fine
For all of our relatives—yours, sir, and mine ;—
So, though greatly disposed at this season to wander
Afloat in the air on my very fine gander,
Instead of such exercise, wholesome and hearty,
I've come with great pleasure to your Christmas party.

Father Christmas (bowing) :

Thanks, thanks, Mother Goose, for the honor you pay
To me your old friend now this many a day ;
Tho' we may not, of course, on all questions agree,
We're alike in our love for the children, you see ;

To give them delight is our greatest of pleasures,
And freely we share with them best of our treasures ;
Our energies each of us constantly bends
To keep our loved title " The Children's Two Friends."

Mother Goose :
Ah, yes, Father Christmas, my jingles and rhymes,
The boys and girls know in far separate climes,
And sometimes I think that your son Santa Claus
Earns me more than my share of the children's applause;
For wherever he goes with his wonderful pack
Santa always has some of my books on his back ;
When from Christmas-eve dreams children's eyelids un-
    loose
Oft they find in their stockings my book, "Mother Goose."

Father Christmas :
'Tis true, my dear madam, that I and my son
Respect most profoundly the work you have done.
The boys from our store-rooms in Christmas-tree Land,
Get the bonbons we make on the Sugar-loaf Strand ;
The children enjoy them,—I cannot deny it,—
But still need your writings as part of their diet ;
Your rhymes, wise and witty, their minds will retain
When their toys and their candy are done,—that is plain!

(Enter Jack, the son of Mother Goose.   He carries a large golden egg.)

Jack : Oh, there you are, Mother Goose, hob-
nobbing with Father Christmas! My goose must
have known there was going to be a reunion of the
Goose and Christmas families! She was so obliging
as to lay another egg in honor of the occasion. You
shall have it, Father Christmas, and may good luck
go with it. (*Hands egg.*)

Father Christmas: Thank you, Jack. That's a
present worth having! I wish my son Santa Claus
had as fine a gift to put in every poor body's stocking. He is out on his rounds now, but expects to
be back, as he said, "before the fun begins."

Jack : Santa's always ready for fun!

Mother Goose (taking Jack's hand, as he stands beside her):

"This, my son Jack,
  Is a smart-looking lad ;
  He is not very good,
  Nor yet very bad."
        (*Sound of voices outside.*)

Jack : Dear me, mother! I can't stir without those young ones following me ! (*Sound of voices and knocking.*)

Children (outside): Jack! Jack!

Jack (calling): All right. Come in. I'm here, and Mother Goose and Father Christmas, too. Surprise us all by being good, won't you ?

(Enter, two by two, Little Bo-Peep with a bundle of lamb's wool suspended from a shepherdess crook ; Little Jack Horner, carrying carefully a deep pan covered with paper pie crust : Little Miss Muffett, carrying a bowl and spoon ; Peter Pumpkin Eater, with a pumpkin under his arm ; Curly Locks, with a piece of needlework : Little Boy Blue, with a Christmas horn ; Contrary Mary, with a string of bells for bracelets, and carrying shells ; Little Tommy Tucker, with a sheet of music ; Jack and Jill, carrying a pail ; Simple Simon, finger in mouth, looking as idiotic as possible : Polly Flinders, in a torn dress, sprinkled with ashes. The children march and countermarch to music around Mother Goose and Father Christmas, bowing as they pass them. When Mother Goose claps her hands the children group themselves on her side of platform, not in a stiff row, but as naturally as possible. As one after another comes forward for his or her speech, the others appear to be conversing among themselves, making the by-play in keeping with their characters.)

Mother Goose : Tell Father Christmas your names now, my pretty ones, and give him the presents you have brought in his honor.

Little Bo-Peep (coming forward) : I'm little Bo-Peep who lost her sheep. I bring you some fine lamb's wool to keep you warm, Father Christmas.

(*Father Christmas receives with a gracious air this gift and those that follow, handing them afterward to Jack Goose, who puts them into a large box or basket previously provided for the purpose.*)

Jack Horner : I'm little Jack Horner who sat in a corner, eating a Christmas pie. I've brought you one just like it, Father Christmas. This pie is full of plums, and I haven't put in my thumb to pull out one! (*Goes back to place after handing pie.*)

Miss Muffet: I'm little Miss Muffet, sir. I sat on a tuffet, eating some curds and whey; but there came a big spider, and I was frightened away. Do you like curds and whey, Father Christmas? I hope so, for here are some in a bowl. (*Hands gift, and returns to place.*)

Peter Pumpkin Eater: Here come I, Peter, Peter, Pumpkin Eater. But I've saved a nice pumpkin for *you*, Father Christmas, and here it is. (*Returns to place.*)

Curly Locks: Just little Curly Locks who sits on a cushion and sews a fine seam, and feeds upon strawberries, sugar, and cream! Here's some of my sewing, Father Christmas. (*Presents needlework, and returns to place.*)

Little Boy Blue (*blowing several blasts on his horn as he comes forward*): Here's Little Boy Blue! I blow my horn when sheep's in the meadow and cow's in the corn. I've brought you my very best horn for a present, Father Christmas. It's a good one, I can tell you! (*Blows again, and hands to Father Christmas, who smilingly tries the horn before handing on to Jack.*)

Contrary Mary: " Mary, Mary, quite contrary," they call me, Father Christmas. I'm not contrary at all. Don't you believe it. Only I *don't* like to do just the same as other folks. That's the reason I'm not going to give you one of my silver bells or my pretty shells. I'll keep them myself for the present. Perhaps when it's Fourth of July, or some other time when nobody else is thinking about giving you anything, you'll hear from Contrary Mary. (*Flounces herself away to place.*)

Mother Goose: Fie, fie, my child! Give your presents to Father Christmas as you should. This contrariness grows upon you apace, and must be checked at once. (*Mary obeys Mother Goose reluctantly, pouting and muttering to herself.*

Little Tommy Tucker: I am only little Tommy Tucker who sings for his supper. All I can give you is a song, Father Christmas.

TOMMY TUCKER'S SONG.

(Air: "Ben Bolt.")

Oh, don't you remember when children were old,
    And money grew up on the trees,
How we lived upon nothing but cake and ice-cream,
    And had none but our own selves to please?
We went to bed late every night of our lives,
    And we played every day all day long;
And we never did sums, and could spell anyhow,
    And nobody said it was wrong!

Oh, don't you remember the naughty child grew,
    The good one was good all in vain,
Till dear Father Christmas and Mother Goose, too,
    To children their duty made plain?
So now we can cipher and spell with a will,
    And at nine we are snug in our beds,
With good Father Christmas in all of our dreams,
    And Mother Goose songs in our heads!

Father Christmas: Bravo, Tom Tucker! Be sure you shall have the supper for which you have sung so well. Bless my eyes! Who comes here?

Jack and Jill (*together*): We are Jack and Jill, Father Christmas. And here's a pail for you. It is the one that we had when " Jack fell down and broke his crown, and Jill came tumbling after." (*Hands a pail.*)

Simple Simon (*drawling*): Simple Simon, I am. I met a pieman going to the fair. Says Simple Simon to the pieman, " Let me taste your fare." Says the pieman to Simple Simon, " Show me first your penny." Says Simple Simon to the pieman, " Indeed, I have not any."

Father Christmas : So you did not get the pie ? My boy, let it be a lesson to you that in this world nobody can have something for nothing.

Polly Flinders (*sobbing*): I don't look fit to come to a party, Father Christmas, for I burnt my best dress sitting among the cinders. Please excuse me this time, and let me stay, though I have no gift.

Father Christmas : Certainly, my dear, certainly.

Mother Goose (*severely*): You are entirely too indulgent, Father Christmas ! Polly Flinders, who sat among the cinders, ought to have stayed at home. (*Polly begins to cry.*)

Father Christmas : Oh, we must overlook her appearance this time, Mother Goose. Christmas is no time for tears. Go back among your brothers and sisters, Polly. Mother Goose and I will let you stay, but don't sit again among the cinders, Polly Flinders !

(Sound of singing outside. Children of All Nations enter, waving flags. At the conclusion of their song they stand in a semicircle behind Father Christmas and Mother Goose.)

SONG OF ALL NATIONS.

(Air: " Upidee," page 68, Franklin Sq. Coll. No. 1.)

Dear Father Christmas, you we greet,
  Tra la la, tra la la,
And Mother Goose, his friend so meet,
  Tra la la, la la.
From every nation on the earth
We hail you both with Christmas mirth.

Chorus.—Merry, merry Christmas, all !
 Christmas gay, happy day !
 Merry, merry Christmas, all !
 Merry Christmas day !

(Pointing to Mother Goose and Father Christmas.)
 " The Children's Friends " their name is known,
 Tra la la, tra la la ;
Oh, long may they that title own,
 Tra la la, la la.
Wherever in the whole wide world
The flag of childhood is unfurled.— *Cho.*

(Taking places.)
 Above our two most loving friends,
 Tra la la, tra la la,
 The banner of each nation bends,
 Tra la la, la la.
 Hurrah for Father Christmas dear !
 And also Mother Goose we'll cheer !—*Cho.*

(Enter Thanksgiving, carrying a basket of fruit, and accompanied by her children, Peace and Plenty.)

Father Christmas : Why, here's my dear niece Thanksgiving, with her two fine youngsters, Peace and Plenty ! Thanksgiving, my dear, permit me to present you to Mother Goose, her son Jack, and all the rest of her family. (*Mutual recognitions.*) Also, to the Children of All Nations. (*Bows.*)

Thanksgiving :
With Peace and with Plenty, my children, I bring
To good Father Christmas our small offering. (*Presents basket.*)

Peace and Plenty (*together*) :
Long live Father Christmas and Mother Goose, too !
Their fame is world-wide, and their friends not a few.

(Thanksgiving, Peace, and Plenty now take places near Father Christmas, while Happy New Year enters, carrying a bunch of keys. She is accompanied by two children, Hope and Good Resolutions.)

Father Christmas (*rising to greet her*): My dear
daughter Happy New Year, we are glad to see you,
with Hope and Good Resolutions looking so bright
and well.   Permit me to introduce my guests.   (*Mutual recognitions.*)

Happy New Year:
   With Good Resolutions quite close to my side,
   And sweet little Hope with me whate'er betide,
   I bring Father Christmas the bright golden keys
   That will open my door '98 with ease.

Hope and Good Resolutions (*together*) :
Good cheer, Mother Goose !   Father Christmas, good
   cheer !
We wish each and all of you happy New Year !

   (Happy New Year and her children group themselves next to Thanksgiving.   Enter Santa Claus, bustling about and shaking hands with everybody while speaking.)

Santa Claus :
What ho, Father Christmas !   What ho, Mother Goose !
At last from my Christmas-eve duties I'm loose.
Not a stocking from north pole to south but I've filled,
Books, candies, and toys by each mantlepiece spilled.
My pack is quite empty, my reindeer done out,
But on Christmas morning there'll be such a shout
From the east to the west, from the south to the north,
When their gifts from their stockings the children pull
      forth,
That it's worth all my trouble—that hearty good cheer,
" Hurrah !   In the night Santa Claus has been here ! "
But, folks, I am hungry, I freely confess,
So on to the dining-room now I will press.
Roast turkey and cranberry sauce and mince pie
Are there on the table, I saw passing by.

Father Christmas :
Now Santa has come, let the banquet be shared
That for our reunion I've ordered prepared.
To the dining-room we will adjourn, Mother Goose ;
                              (*Takes her arm.*)

Come, all the rest, follow—I'll take no excuse.
Santa Claus, lead Thanksgiving ; Jack, Happy New Year;
Away now, my friends, to our good Christmas cheer !

(All go out, two by two, singing the following stanza to the air of
"Upidee.")

All together :

Come to the Christmas feast so gay,
 Tra la la, tra la la ;
Good Father Christmas leads the way,
 Tra la la, la la.
Come, children, he'll " take no excuse ; "
Come, follow him and Mother Goose.

Merry, merry Christmas, all !
 Christmas gay, happy day !
Merry, merry Christmas, all,
 Merry Christmas day.

Christmas Waits.

By KATHERINE WEST.

(Dress four boys, or six, in a quaint costume,—full knee-breeches, low
shoes with bright buckles, tunic or doublet with white frills at the throat
and wrist ; a short full cape hanging from the shoulders, and soft caps
with plumes. Old garments may be re-arranged to give a picturesque
effect, or some new, inexpensive material bought. Each boy should have
a voice of pleasing quality, and be taught the Christmas song perfectly.

Arrange a frame like a window casement at the back of the platform a
little to one side. Behind this let a light burn dimly until a signal is
given for full illumination. If practicable, leave the rest of the stage and
audience-room in darkness.

The boys begin to sing behind closed doors, and are heard coming
nearer singing the first verse of "On this Happy Birthday." They enter
and approach the centre of the platform. The casement is thrown open
and half a dozen children's heads appear. There is a clapping of hands
till the second verse is begun by the waits. At the last line the children
throw out pennies and candies wrapped in paper. The singers scramble
for them, and then give the third verse of the carol. The fourth verse
may be sung as the boys move away and disappear in the distance. As a
preliminary to this little performance a few words may be said about the
old English custom of the waits coming to sing under the windows on
Christmas eve.)

ON THIS HAPPY BIRTHDAY.

Mrs. CHARLOTTE B. MERRITT.

Mrs. SARAH L. WARNER.

1. On this happy Birthday Of our Saviour King, Come, dear little children, Sweetly let us sing
2. Bethlehem's star is shining, Ho - ly is its ray, To the world proclaiming Christ was born to-day.
3. Wise men came to worship, Wise men from a-far, Guided by the glo - ry Of that ho - ly star.

Of the Christ Child; Of the Christ Child, We will glad - ly sing.
Of the Christ Child, Of the Christ Child, We will glad - ly sing.
Of the Christ Child, Of the Christ Child, We will glad - ly sing.

4.
Now He reigns forever,
Loving you and me;
Joyful, let us praise Him
Round our Christmas tree.
To the Christ Child,
To the Christ Child,
We our tribute bring.

COPYRIGHT 1876. BY BIGLOW & MAIN.

A Christmas Party.

By Lizzie M. Hadley.

(CHARACTERS: *1897*, a bent and feeble old man with skull-cap and white beard, leaning on a cane. The number 1897 across his forehead or breast. *South Wind*, a slender brunette in veil, mantle, and cape of green cheese cloth, cape belted down in the back. As she enters she flourishes her arms to throw out veil and cape. *Messenger*, in lettered uniform. Four *Heralds*, uniformed somewhat like messenger. Nine *Fairies*, very small girls. Corenets of silver paper. Flowing robes of cheese cloth with angel sleeves worn over clothing sufficiently warm for the season. Colors to represent the plants whose leaves they carry. Silver belts, shoe-buckles, and necklaces. Leaves cut from green paper, and letters from gilt. *Kriss Kringle, Santa Claus, St. Nicholas, Knight Rupert*, and *Babousca* in appropriate costumes. Nine *Children*, in ordinary clothes. *North Wind, East Wind*, and *West Wind* in costumes similar to *South Wind*, but varying in color,—white for north, blue for east, and red for west. The Winds stand behind St. Nicholas and keep up a restless blowing; that is, a fluttering and ballooning of capes and veils by flourishing arms.)

1897 : I'm growing old and feeble,
　　So much excitement's wrong ;
Folks should have had their Christmas
　　When I was young and strong.
Instead of that, they take it
　　When I really ought to rest.
My last days should be peaceful
　　But—Father Time knows best.

And now I must be stirring,
　　And call for Santa Claus ;
I almost dread his coming,
　　There's always such a noise.
The winds shall be my heralds—
　　Come, North Wind, where are you ?
Just whisper to old Santa
　　That here he'll soon be due.

Now while I am about it,
　　Perhaps it would be best
To call that windy herald
　　Whose home is in the west.
　　　　(*Enter South Wind.*)
Here comes my daughter, South Wind.

South Wind :
   I'm almost out of breath,
    I really fear the North Wind
   Intends to be my death.

 1897 : I'll bid him treat you kindly ;
    He should not be so rough ;
   He's getting much too boisterous,
    I know that well enough.
   You're all here now but East Wind
    I'll call for him again.

Messenger (*entering*) :
   The East Wind says his health demands
    A little snow or rain.
 1897 : Well, well, just tell the storm clouds
    To send us rain or snow.

(*Snowflakes begin to fall, seen through a window,—cot-
ton or bits of paper.*)
   Well done !   Now are you ready
    Upon your way to go ?
   For some one must be bidding
    Knight Rupert come this way,
   To give the German children
    Their presents, Christmas day.
   And then there's old Babousca—
    In Russia she'll be found ;
   Kriss Kringle and St. Nicholas,
    They, too, must both be round.

Heralds : We know where each one liveth,
    Full soon they shall appear.
   We go to do your bidding.
    Farewell, farewell, Old Year.
    (*Exit Heralds.   Enter Fairies.*)

 1897 : Bless me ! what little people !
    (*Speaks to first one.*)
   Why, who are you, my dear ?
   I ne'er before have seen you.
   What are you doing here ?

Fairies : Oh, we are little fairies
From out the ether blue.
Here is a Christmas posy
We are bringing unto you.
And the initial letters
Will a starry chaplet make.
Each trusts you will receive it,
And wear it for her sake.

First Fairy (pointing to first leaf in chaplet) :
This is for **C**ypress.
Second Fairy : And this for **H**olly.
Third Fairy : And this for **R**ose of Jericho.
Fourth Fairy : And this for **I**vy.
Fifth Fairy : And this for **S**peedwell.
Sixth Fairy : And this for **T**hyme.
Seventh Fairy : And this for **M**istletoe.
Eighth Fairy : And this for
the quivering **A**spen.
Ninth Fairy : And this for **S**tar of Bethlehem.
(*They place chaplet upon the head of* 1897.)
1897 : Here's thanks, my little people,
For this your posy sweet ;
Your loving thought has surely
Made my happiness complete.

(*Enter Kriss Kringle, Santa Claus, Prince Rupert*, and
Babousca.)

> Why here is old Kriss Krinkle ;
>   And Santa's coming, too ;
> Knight Rupert and Babousca,
>   I welcome both of you.
> And from the frozen Northland,
>   I see a-riding down

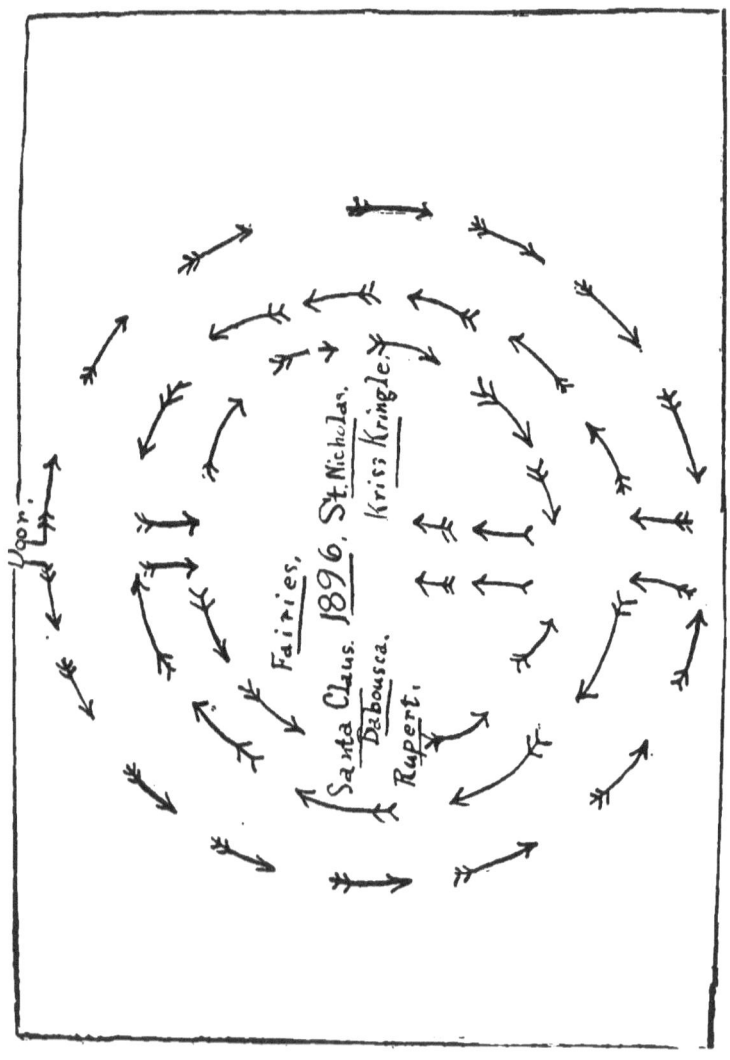

The cheery old St. Nicholas,
Clad in his friar's gown.

(*Enter St. Nicholas.*)

(*Enter children, singing.   They march around the stage,
and finally stop in front of 1897 and the others.*)

See how the children, so happy and gay,
Come marching together this glad Christmas day.

Children :

With hands on our heads, while the bells sweetly chime,
All blithely we're keeping the glad Christmas time.
Marching and singing, so gayly we go,
Turning and winding in lines to and fro.
Clap all together, and sing, sing away,
So merrily keeping this glad Christmas day.

1897 : Oh, children, little children,
            You're welcome here alway ;
        I'm glad to see you coming
            To keep our Christmas day.
            (*Bells outside.*)
        Oh, children, little children,
            Why do the joy-bells chime ?

(*Singing heard outside.   The following words, to the
tune of "Ring, Ye Happy Christmas Bells."*)

        Carol, O ye children all,
            With no thought of sadness ;
        Welcome in the Christmas time
            With your songs of gladness.

    Chorus.—Sing, O sing,
            Bells all ring,
            Let us now be merry,
            Let us welcome Christmas day
            With our songs so cheery.

1897 : Hark, how the winds are blowing,
            What music do they bring.

Children : You hear the little children
Their Christmas carols sing.

1897 : O children, little children,
What light is that afar ?

Children : 'Tis shining from the heavens,
A glorious Christmas star.

1897 : O children, little children,
What means its glorious rays ?
And why is Christmas better
Than many other days ?

Children : Oh, don't you know the story
Of the first Christmas time ?
Then listen, we will tell it,
While the bells so sweetly chime.

First child : We count the years by hundreds
Since that first Christmas day,
When in a lowly manger
The little Christ-child lay.

Second child : That night some shepherds tending
Their flocks upon the hill,
Heard heavenly voices singing,
" Peace, peace !   On earth, good will."

Third child : All bright as noon-tide splendor.
A light about them shone,
While louder sang the angels,
" A Saviour hath been born ! "

Fourth child : And then a sudden darkness—
The voices died away,
The wondering shepherds hurried
To where the young Child lay.

Fifth child : Their flocks were all untended,
While filled with love and awe,
They bent above the manger
And the Baby Jesus saw.

Sixth child : Then, too, the wise men watching
Beheld a star that shone,
In the blue heavens above them
To tell that Christ was born.

Seventh child : And with their camels laden
With spices and gold.
They came from eastern countries
The young King to behold.

Eighth child : The star still went before them,
And pointing out the way,
It shone upon the stable
Where the Babe of Bethlehem **lay**

Ninth child : And then, all lowly bending,
They worshipped the young King,
And gave him from their treasures
Full many an offering.

Santa Claus, St. Nicholas, Kriss Kringle, etc. :
O children we have numbered
Long centuries since then,
But we see at every Christmas
That little Child again.
And we bring to all good children
In memory of that time,
Some pretty Christmas present,
While the joy-bells gayly chime.

1897 : O children, little children,
I soon must pass away,
But 'tis good to have the memory
Of this blessed Christmas day.

Santa Claus and others :
We, too, must now be going,
And as we march along,
O let us sing together
A happy Christmas song.

(*All march out singing.   Tune "Yankee Doodle."*)
O the merry Christmas time
Now is in the way, sir,
Ev'ry sweet and happy chime
Tells of Christmas day, sir.

Chorus.—Christmas it is coming, now,
Don't you hear the bells, sir?
Happy Christmas time is here,
To the world we tell, sir.

Santa's Helpers.

By M. Nora Boylan.

The fairies and brownies on last Christmas-tide
Decided to open their hearts very wide,
And spend extra time, throughout the whole year,
In helping their grandfather—Santa Claus dear.

" Our fingers are nimble.   We'll quickly make toys
Enough to supply all the girls and the boys,
And Santa may watch us to see if it's right,
So all will be ready before Christmas night."

Then bravely they all went to work with a will,
And soon all was quiet in workshop and mill ;
For old Santa said, " Enough, and well done,
We've toys enough now to make all kinds of fun."

We thank you, old Santa, and your helpers, too,
For all of the many kind things that you do ;
And should you need more help in making your toys,
Just call on your small friends, the girls and the boys.

Christmas Eve.

(This must be spoken as if singing a lullaby to a baby, with motions
indicating the sleeping child near.)

Oh, hush thee, little dear, my soul,
    The evening shades are falling ;
Hush thee, my dear, dost thou not hear
    The voice of the Master calling ?

Deep lies the snow upon the earth,
    But all the sky is ringing
With joyous song, and all night long
    The stars shall dance with singing.

Oh, hush thee, little dear, my soul,
    And close thine eyes in dreaming,
And angels fair shall lead thee where
    The singing stars are beaming.

A shepherd calls his little lambs,
    And he longeth to caress them ;
He bids them rest upon his breast,
    That his tender love may bless them.

So, hush thee, little dear, my soul,
    Whilst evening shades are falling,
And above the song of the heavenly throng
    Thou shalt hear the Master calling.
                —*Eugene Field.*

Santa Claus's Visit.

By Susie M. Best.

With a click and a clack
And a great big pack,
Down through the chimney,
Pretty nimbly
Somebody comes on Christmas eve !

If we are real nice
And as still as mice,
If we never peep,
And are sound asleep,
He'll fill our stockings, I do believe !

And when we arise
Next day our eyes
Will grow big to see
How perfectly
He knew what we all wished to receive !

To Santa Claus.

By JENNIE D. MOORE.

(Recitation for a little boy.)

Dear Santa Claus, I'll let you know
  The few things that I need,
And if you'll bring them to me
  I'll be much obliged indeed.

I want a horse and wagon,
  And a boat that's painted red,
An elephant, a jumping-jack—
  You need not bring a sled,

For I have one very pretty ;
  But I want a trotting-horse,
A man who wheels a wheel-barrow,
  And candy, too, of course.

Now, Santa dear, you'll not forget.
  I wish you'd write them down,
And leave them all at my house
  When you journey through the town.

What I Should Like.

By JENNIE D. MOORE.

(Recitation for a little girl.)

On Christmas eve I'd like to lie
Awake, when stars are in the sky,
And listen to the sound that swells
From Santa Claus's jingling bells.

I'd like to hear upon the roof
The patter of each tiny hoof
Of Santa's reindeer overhead,
When I am snug and warm in bed.

But mamma says I must not lie
Awake, or he will pass me by ;
He does not like the girls or boys
To watch him when he brings the **toys.**

I think I'd better go to sleep.
I guess the presents all will keep,
Then in the morning I shall be
Glad to think I did not see.

A Gentle Reminder.

Something new about Christmas ?
    Why, what were half so sweet
As the old, old way of keeping
    The day our glad hearts greet ?

The old, old chimes are dearest;
    The old, old songs are best ;
It's the old, old gladness welling
    Within each joyous breast.

Then my little lad said slyly,
    " Remember, if that's true,
That your old, old way, mamma dear,
    Was to give *me* something new."

Alice W. Rollins.

Christmas Time.

By M. N. B.

(An introductory recitation for a Christmas program.)

Christmas time for boys and girls,
  Is a happy day,
For we go to grandmamma's
  And eat and sing and play.

Grandma does not say to us—
  "Stop that horrid noise,"
'Cause she understands we can't,
  When we're " *only boys.*"

And she lets the girls play house,
  In the garret old,
And when they strew things around,
  Grandma doesn't scold.

But we ought to pick them up,
  Even on Christmas day,
For we shouldn't make kind friends
  Trouble with our play.

Yes, we love the Christmas time
  Best of all the year,
We have waited for it long,
  Now, at last, it's here.

Christmas Wishes.

By C. PHILLIPS.

(These couplets may be given by three primary children to open a
Christmas program.)

First child :
  Dear teachers and friends, allow me to say
  That we wish you a very glad Christmas day.

Second child :
> That our darling old " Santa," as sly as a fox,
> May leave at your door both bundle and box.

Third child :
> And that beautiful gifts for one and for all
> From the evergreen boughs may happily fall !

Christmas Morn.

By M. N. B.

(Recitation and chorus.   A semi-circle of primary children is ,ormed on
he stage. They sing first verse of the familiar church tune, " Joy to the
world.")

Chorus.—Joy to the world, the Lord has come,
> Let earth receive her King,
> Let every heart prepare him room,
> And heaven and nature sing.

Recitation (one child steps forward).—
> In Bethlehem, the story goes,
> A little Child was born,
> Low in a manger He was laid
> The first glad Christmas morn.

> That Child is now our Saviour King,
> Of Him we sing to-day ;
> And may glad bells o'er all the earth
> Ring out a gladsome lay.

Chorus.—Joy to the world, a Saviour reigns,
> Let men their tongues employ,
> While fields and floods, rocks, hills, and vales
> Repeat the sounding joy.

My Christmas Secrets.

By S. C. PEABODY.

Hurry Christmas ! How you creep !
I've some presents I can't keep,
Just this morning I forgot,
And told baby what I'd bought.

All he answered was, " Goo goo ! "
So I don't think that he knew,
I told mamma hers was white,
And she'd wear it every night.

That she'd need it getting tea.
Then my mamma smiled at me,
And she whispered, " Isn't May
Letting secrets fly away ? "

Kriss Kringle.

By Susie M. Best.

If there's any one here who ever has seen
The face of Kriss Kringle, I'll think he is mean
If he is not willing at once to arise
And tell the real color and shape of his eyes !

Somehow I much doubt if the gentleman looks
Like the pictures we see in the shops and the books.
I've a sort of a notion we'd all be surprised
If we suddenly saw him, by day, undisguised !

Is he big, is he little, is he young, is he old ?
There are some things, I know, that can't always be told,
But I'd much like to know why it is he must keep
Himself hidden securely till we are asleep ?

I've made up my mind that I'm going to watch,
And see if I cannot by any means catch
One glimpse of his face as he comes down the flue,
And if I succeed I'll describe him to you !

A Message.

By Ella M. Powers.

(For three primary children to recite.)

First pupil : One true thing I have to say,
Clap your hands now, for you may.
It's very happy, very dear,
This Christmas day will soon be h᷉ re ;
But children learn to understand,
That loyal heart and loving hand,
Can pray, " Oh, Saviour, so divine,
Make our lives so much like thine."

Second pupil : Yes, far away that Christmas night,
A star above the Christ shone bright,
And led the shepherds from afar
To seek that bright and glorious star.

Third pupil : The shepherds came with presents rare
And knelt with tender love and care,
Before that child so sweet and true,
And loved Him as we all should do ;
And that grand song we hear again,
" Peace on earth—good will to men."

The Mousie.

By M. N. B.

(A very small primary boy may recite these lines.)

A mousie got into a great Christmas pie,
Two little boys heard him, and then they did cry,
" O mousie ! O mousie ! come quickly away !
That pie is not for you, 'tis for our Christmas day.

A Letter from Santa Claus.

By William Howard.

(A little girl is seated with her slate and pencil. A postman's whistle is heard, and she exclaims, "There is the letter-man!" She runs to the door and returns with a large envelope, made of white wrapping-paper sealed with red wax, which she tears open, announces it is written by Santa Claus to the pupils of the school, and then reads it aloud. In the last verse the names of the children present are to be substituted for the printed ones.)

Merry Christmas! little children,
    From my home so far away
Send I loving Christmas greetings
    To you on your holiday.

You may watch and wait till midnight,
    Looking at the falling snow,
But be sure you won't discover
    When I come or when I go.

For I come when all is silent,
    Not a breath will then be heard,
And I softly through the chimney
    Enter, saying not a word.

Quickly to the stockings step I,
    And I place in every one
Something for the Christmas frolic,
    Something for the Christmas fun.

Hark! my reindeer out the window,
    Prance and shake a warning note;
Santa Claus will speed away then,
    Wrapping close his cap and coat.

Your surprise, when comes the morning,
    Gladness which your bright eyes tell,
Grateful, merry, happy children,
    Pleases Santa Claus full well.

Willie, Alice, Harry, Mary,
    Christmas greetings now I send.
Cora, Freddie, Sadie, Johnnie,
    Don't forget Santa Claus, your friend.

The Christmas We Like.

By ELLA M. POWERS.

(A recitation for two primary children.)

First pupil: Just a little stocking,
Very small indeed,
Hang it by the chimney,
Santa Claus will heed.

Then on Christmas morning
I will run and see
All the lovely presents
He has left for me.

Second pupil: I never think that Christmas
Is quite so full of joy,
Unless I find a poor child
And give her a nice toy.

For don't you know at Christmas
We must be happy then,
And love to do for others
As Christ did to all men.

Saint Nick.

By M. N. B.

(For the youngest pupil to recite.)

When cold the winds blow,
And comes the white snow,
Then look out for good Saint Nick.
He comes in a sleigh
From miles, miles away,
And vanishes very quick.

Merry, Merry Christmas.

(Over the platform against the wall hang the words " Merry, Merry Christmas." They may be simply made of dark-colored pasteboard twelve inches high, or the cardboard may be covered with red berries and ever-green. The five children who recite in turn point to the words whenever they speak them.)

First child : Oh ! " merry, merry Christmas,"
            Blithely let us sing,
            And " merry, merry Christmas,"
            Let the church-bells ring.
                Lo ! the little stranger,
                Smiling in the manger
            Is the King of Kings.

Second child : Oh ! " merry, merry Christmas,"
            Weave in fragrant green,
            And " merry, merry Christmas,"
            In holly-berries' sheen.
                Opened heaven's portals,
                That by favored mortals
            Angels might be seen.

Third child : Oh ! " merry, merry Christmas,"
            Carol bright and gay,
            For " merry, merry Christmas "
            Is the Children's day ;
                Morning stars revealing
                Shepherds humbly kneeling
            Where the Christ child lay.

Fourth child : Oh ! " merry, merry Christmas,"
            Day of sacred mirth ;
            Oh! merry, merry Christmas,"
            Sing the Saviour's birth.
                Christ, the high and holy,
                Once so meek and lowly,
            Came from heaven to earth.

Fifth child: Oh ! " merry, merry Christmas,"
Shout the happy sound,
Till " merry, merry Christmas,"
Spreads the world around ;
Wonderful the story,
Unto God may glory
Evermore abound.
Carine L. Rose, in Good Housekeeping.

Christmas Questions.

BY WOLSTAN DIXEY.

(At the three last words the speaker raises her finger impressively.)

How old is Santa Claus ?   Where does he keep ?
And why does he come when I am asleep ?
His hair is so white in the pictures I know,
Guess he stands on his head all the time in the snow.
But if he does that, then why don't he catch cold ?
He must be as much as,—most twenty years old.
I'd just like to see him once stand on his head,
And dive down the chimney, as grandmother said.
Why don't his head get all covered with black ?
And if he comes head first, how can he get back ?
Mamma knows about it, but she wont tell me.
I shall keep awake Christmas eve, then I can see.
I have teased her to tell me, but mamma she won't,
So I'll find out myself now ; see if I don't.

A Catastrophe

BY SUSIE M. BEST.

If old Kriss Kringle should forget
To travel Christmas eve,
I tell you now, I think next day
The little folks would grieve.

There wouldn't be a single toy,
  A single box or book,
And not a bit of candy in
  Their stockings when they'd look.

Because, you see, Kriss Kringle has
  A " corner " on these things,
'Tis he, and he alone, who in
  The night our presents brings.

Then let us all try to avert
  This sad catastrophe,
And hope Kriss Kringle may at least
  Remember you and me.

A Christmas Gift.

By Mabel L. Pray.

It seems that dear old Santa Claus
  One day in old November
Received a note from Dottie D—,
  With words and phrases tender,
In which she asked the dear old man,
  With many words of warning,
To bring her a new Paris doll
  On the next Christmas morning.

Just as he started for his sleigh
  One eve, in old December,
He turned to Mistress Santa Claus
  And said, " Did you remember
About that fine new Paris doll
  For wee Dot in the city ?
I must not fail to take that gift,
  'Twould be a dreadful pity."

It was early in the morning,
  One day in old December ;
A very happy, joyous day
  That children all remember,

When Santa, on his mission fleet,
  To the nursery came creeping,
And left the fine new Paris doll
  Among the others, sleeping.

The holly and the mistletoe
  Were bright this winter morning ;
One stocking filled from top to toe
  The mantel was adorning.
A Christmas tree hung full with gifts,
  While underneath, reposing
On an upholstered rocking chair,
  The Paris doll was dozing.

Then suddenly from out the gloom
  Dot's other dolls came peeping,
Their hair uncombed, their dresses torn,
  And noses red with weeping ;
They talked in whispers soft and low,
  But tones that grew quite scornful,
About the fate that was to greet
  This stranger, sad and mournful.

There were Annabel and Bessie,
  That came one cold December ;
They hobbled round with broken backs
  From falling on the fender.
Then Tommy, Grace, and baby Ruth,
  All came one birthday party,
And Rose and Don a year ago,
  With Santa Claus so hearty.

They all assembled round the tree,
  And then with manners shocking
They pinched and shook the Paris doll,
  And cried in words so mocking--
" Why, don't you know, you stupid thing,
  Dot won't care for another,
She has received this Christmas morn
  A dear, sweet baby brother ! "

A Christmas Thought.

(To be recited with carefu regard to smoothness, without a sing-song
effect.)

Oh Christmas is coming again, you say,
    And you long for the thing: he is bringing ;
But the costliest gift may not gladden the day,
    Nor help on the merry bells ringing
Some getting is losing, you understand,
    Some hoarding is far from saving ;
What you hold in your hand may slip from your hand ;
    There is something better than having ;
        We are richer for what we give ;
        And only by giving we live.

Your last year's presents are scattered and gone ;
    You have almost forgot who gave them ;
But the loving thoughts you bestow live on
    As long as you choose to have them.
Love, love is your riches, though ever so poor ;
    No money can buy that treasure ;
Yours always, from robber and rust secure,
    Your own, without stint or measure :
        It is only love that we can give ;
        It is only by loving we live.

For who is it smiles through the Christmas morn—
    The Light of the wide creation ?
A dear little Child in a stable born,
    Whose love is the world's salvation.
He was poor on earth, but He gave us all
    That can make our life worth the living ;
And happy the Christmas day we call
    That is spent, for His sake, in giving :
        He shows us the way to live,
        Like Him, let us love and give !
                                    —*Lucy Larcom*

A Merry Christmas Eve.

It chanced upon the merry, merry Christmas eve
    I went sighing past the church across the moorland
        dreary :
"Oh ! never sin and want and woe this earth will leave,
    And the bells but mock the wailing round, they sing
        so cheery.
How long, O Lord ! how long before Thou come again ?
    Still in cellar, and in garret, and on moorland dreary
The orphans moan, and widows weep, and poor men
        toil in vain,
    Till earth is full of hope deferred, though Christmas
        bells be cheery."

Then arose a joyous clamor from the wild fowl on the
        mere,
    Beneath the stars, across the snow, like clear bells
        ringing,
And a voice within cried : " Listen !—Christmas carols
        even here !
    Though thou be dumb, yet o'er their work the stars
        and snows are singing.
Blind ! I live, I love, I reign ; and all the nations through
    With the thunder of my judgments even now are
        ringing ;
Do thou fulfill thy work, but as yon wild fowl do,
    Thou wilt hear no less the wailing, yet hear through it
        angels singing."
                    —*Charles Kingsley.*

The Christmas Stocking.

In the ghostly light I'm sitting, musing of long dead
        Decembers,
While the fire-clad shapes are flitting in and out among
        the embers

On my hearthstone in mad races, and I marvel, for in
     seeming
I can dimly see the faces and the scenes of which I'm
     dreaming.

O golden Christmas days of yore !
     In sweet anticipation
I lived their joys for days before
     Their glorious realization ;
          And on the dawn
          Of Christmas morn
My childish heart was knocking
          A wild tattoo,
          As 'twould break through,
As I unhung my stocking.

Each simple gift that came to hand,
     How marvelous I thought it !
A treasure straight from wonderland,
     For Santa Claus had brought it.
          And at my cries
          Of glad surprise
The others all came flocking
          To share my glee
          And view with me
The contents of the stocking

Years sped—I left each well-loved scene
     In Northern wilds to roam,
And there, 'mid tossing pine-trees green,
     I made myself a home.
          We numbered three
          And blithe were we,
At adverse fortune mocking,
          And Christmas-tide
          By our fireside
Found hung the baby's stocking.

Alas ! within our home to-night
     No sweet young voice is ringing,
And through its silent rooms no light,
     Free, childish step is springing.

The wild winds rave
O'er baby's grave
Where plumy pines are rocking
And crossed at rest
On marble breast
The hands that filled my stocking

With misty eyes but steady hand
I raise my Christmas chalice ;
Here's to the children of the land
In cabin or in palace ;
May each one hold
The key of gold,
The gates of glee unlocking,
And hands be found
The whole world round
To fill the Christmas stocking.

—*Clarence H. Pearson in The Ladies' Home Journal.*

Christmas Hymn.

(During this recitation let the piano be played very softly in running chords that resolve into the key of a Christmas carol which is
taken up and sung by the entire school at the end of the poem.)

Sing, Christmas bells !
Say to the earth this is the morn
Whereon our Saviour-King is born ;
Sing to all men—the bond, the free,
The rich, the poor, the high, the low,
The little child that sports in glee,
The aged folk that tottering go,—
Proclaim the morn
That Christ is born,
That saveth them and saveth me !

Sing angel host !
  Sing of the stars that God has placed
Above the manger in the east.
  Sing of the glories of the night,
The Virgin's sweet humility,
  The Babe with kingly robes bedight,—
Sing to all men where'er they be
    This Christmas morn
    For Christ is born,
That saveth them and saveth me !

           —*Eugene Field.*

Bells Across the Snow.

(This poem may be recited by one pupil, or divided as follows :)

First pupil :   Christmas, merry Christmas !
      Is it really come again ?
    With its memories and greetings,
      With its joys and with its pain ;
    There's a minor in the carol,
      And a shadow in the light,
    And a spray of cypress twining
      With the holly wreath to-night.
    And the hush is never broken
      By laughter, light and low,
    As we listen in the starlight
      To the " bells across the snow."

Second pupil :   Christmas, merry Christmas !
      'Tis not so very long
    Since other voices blended
      With the carol and the song !
    If we could but hear them singing
      As they are singing now,
    If we could but see the radiance
      Of the crown on each dear brow :
    There would be no sigh to smother,
      No hidden tear to flow,
    As we listen in the starlight
      To the " bells across the snow."

Third pupil :   O Christmas, merry Christmas !
          This never more can be ;
    We cannot bring again the days
        Of our unshadowed glee.
    But Christmas, happy Christmas,
        Sweet herald of good will,
    With holy songs of glory,
        Brings holy gladness still.
    For peace and hope may brighten,
        And patient love may glow,
    As we listen in the starlight
        To the " bells across the snow."
                —*F. R. Havergal.*

Christmas Eve.

Outside my window whirls the icy storm,
    And beats upon its panes with fingers white ;
Within, my open fire burns bright and warm,
    And sends throughout the room its ruddy light.

Low on the hearth my good grimalkin lies,
    His supple, glossy limbs outstretched along ;
Now gently sleeps with softly closèd eyes,
    Now, half awakened, purrs his even-song.

Near to the fire, touched by its gentle heat,
    A silent, welcome friend, my armchair stands.
Its cushioned depths invite me to its seat,
    And promise rest for weary head and hands.

Within its depths mine eyes unheeded close,
    And comes to me a vision wondrous sweet.
Such sights and sounds no wakeful hours disclose
    As then my resting, dreaming senses greet.

I am where gentle shepherds on the plain
    Keep sleepless, faithful watch o'er resting sheep ;
I hear them chant the Psalmist's sweet refrain,
    That Israel's God will sure his promise keep.

Then quick the air is full of heav'nly song,
    And radiant light illumines all the ground,
While angel voices sweet the strain prolong,
    And angel faces shine in glory round.

I see the shepherds' faces pale with fear,
    Then glow with joy and glad surprise, for then
" Glory to God ! " from angel lips they hear,
    And " Peace on earth good will to men."

And then the light marks out a shining way,
    And swift the shepherds are the path to take.
I long to go · O laggard feet, why stay ?
    Alas ! the vision fades, and I awake.

Within, the smold'ring fire is burning dim ;
    Without, the whirl and beat of storm have ceased.
I still can hear the angels' peaceful hymn,
    And know the vision hath my peace increased.
          — *Frank E. Brown in The Outlook.*

The Little Christmas Tree

The Christmas day was coming, the Christmas eve drew
    near,
The fir-trees they were talking low at midnight cold and
    clear
And this is what the fir-trees said, all in the pale moon-
    light,
" Now which of us shall chosen be to grace the holy
    night ? "

The tall trees and the goodly trees raised each a lofty
    head.
In glad and secret confidence, though not a word they
    said
But one, the baby of the band, could not restrain a sigh—
" You all will be approved," he said, " but, oh ! what
    chance have I ? "

Then axe on shoulder, to the grove a woodman took his
  way.
One baby-girl he had at home, and he went forth to find
A little tree as small as she, just suited to his mind.

Oh, glad and proud the baby-fir, amid its brethren tall,
To be thus chosen and singled out, the first among them
  all !
He stretched his fragrant branches, his little heart beat
  fast,
He was a real Christmas tree ; he had his wish at last.

One large and shining apple with cheeks of ruddy gold,
Six tapers, and a tiny doll were all that he could hold.

" I am so small, so very small, no one will mark or know
How thick and green my needles are, how true my
  branches grow ;
Few toys and candles could I hold, but heart and will
  are free,
And in my heart of hearts I know I am a Christmas
  tree."

The Christmas angel hovered near ; he caught the
  grieving word,
And, laughing low, he hurried forth, with love and pity
  stirred.
He sought and found St Nicholas, the dear old Christmas saint,
And in his fatherly kind ear rehearsed the fir-tree's
  plaint.

Saints are all-powerful, we know, so it befell that day,
The baby laughed, the baby crowed, to see the tapers
  bright ;
The forest baby felt the joy, and shared in the delight.

And when at last the tapers died, and when the baby
  slept,
The little fir in silent night a patient vigil kept ;
Though scorched and brown its needles were, it had no
  heart to grieve.
" I have not lived in vain," he said ; "thank God for
  Christmas eve ! "

—*Susan Coolidge.*

The Russian Santa Claus.

By Lizzie M. Hadley.

Over the Russian snows one day,
Upon the eve of a Christmas day,
While still in the heavens shone afar,
Like a spark of fire, that wondrous star,
Three kings with jewels and gold bedight
Came journeying on through the wintry night.

Out of the East they rode amain,
With servants and camels in their train.
Laden with spices, myrrh, and gold,
Gems and jewels of worth untold,
Presents such as to-day men bring,
To lay at the feet of some Eastern king.

Wrinkled and feeble, old and gray,
Dame Babousca, that Christmas day,
Looked from her hut beside the moor,
Where the four roads crossed by her cottage door,
And saw the kings on their camels white,
A shadowy train in the wintry night.

They knocked at her cabin door to tell
That wonderful story we know so well,
Of the star that was guiding them all the way
To the place where the little Christ-Child lay,
And they begged that she, through the sleet and snow,
To the nearest village with them would go.

But naught cared she for that unknown Child,
And winds about her blew fierce and wild,
For the night was stormy, dark, and cold,
And poor Babousca was weak and old,
And in place of the pitiless winter's night,
Her lowly hut seemed a palace bright.

So to their pleadings she answered " Nay,"
And watched them all as they rode away

But when they had gone and the night was still,
Her hut seemed lonely, and dark, and chill,
And she almost wished she had followed them
In search of the Babe of Bethlehem.

And then as the longing stronger grew,
She said, "I will find Him," but no one knew,
Where was the cradle in which He lay
When He came to earth upon Christmas day,
For the kings and their trains were long since gone,
And none could tell of the Babe, new born.

Then filling a basket with toys, she said,
As over the wintry moor she sped,
"I will go to the busy haunts of men,
There I shall find the kings, and then,
Together we'll go that Child to meet,
And jewels and toys we'll lay at His feet.

The kings with their trains have long been clay,
The hut on the moor has mouldered away,
But old and feeble, worn and gray,
Every year upon Christmas day,
It matters not though the winds blow chill,
Old Babousca is seeking still.

And every year when the joy-bells chime,
To tell of the blessed Christmas time,
When in Holland they tell to the girls and boys,
Of good Saint Nicholas and his toys,
In Russia, the little children say,
"Old Babousca has passed this way."

A Christmas Garden.

(A prose recitation, or suggestion for composition.)

There is a story told of a magician who conjured up a garden in the winter time. The wand of the wizard, however, is not necessary to dislose even in a northern climate in the cold months the beautiful contents of Nature's world. The varieties of evergreen, pine, hemlock, fir, cedar, and larch provide a variety of green foliage through the dreary weather. The rich, clustering berries, besides their ornamental character, furnish food for the snowbirds. The Christmas rose, wax-like in its white purity, will bloom out of doors long after frost if a glass is turned over the plant on cold nights. The ivy remains glossy, its green berry another addition to our winter bouquet.

Farther south, but still within our United States, the scarlet holly grows in luxuriance. So full of holiday association is this tree that its branches are carefully transported a thousand miles for use during Christmas week. Its crisp leaves, lively color, and happy sentiment make the holly, pre-eminent as a winter ornament, prince in our Christmas garden.

A contrast is furnished by the delicate sprays of the mistletoe growing upon the limbs of the oak, elm, and apple trees. The white berry attaches itself, curiously enough, without roots of any kind, and becomes an enduring plant.

A Christmas Carol.

" What means this glory round our feet?"
  The Magi mused, " more bright than morn?"
And voices chanted clear and sweet,
  " To-day the Prince of Peace is born!"

" What means that star?" the shepherd said,
  " That brightens through the rocky glen?"
And angels answering overhead,
  Sang, " Peace on earth, good will to men!"

'Tis eighteen hundred years and more
  Since those sweet oracles were dumb ;
We wait for Him, like them of yore ;
  Alas, He seems so slow to come !

But it was said, in words of gold,
  No time or sorrow e'er shall dim,
That little children might be bold
  In perfect trust to come to Him.

All round about our feet shall shine
  A light like that the wise men saw,
If we our loving wills incline
  To that sweet Life which is the Law.

So shall we learn to understand
  The simple faith of shepherds then,
And clasping kindly hand in hand,
  Sing, " Peace on earth, good will to men ! "

And they who do their souls no wrong,
  But keep at eve the faith of morn,
Shall daily hear the angel-song,
  " To-day the Prince of Peace is born ! "
                              —*J. R. Lowell.*

The Power of Christmas.

Even under the pressure of battle the influence
of the Christmas season has exerted a powerful
effect.   In 1428, during the war of the roses, while
Orleans was under siege, the English lords, history
tells us, requested the French commanders to sus-
pend hostilities, and let the usual celebration of
Christmas eve take their place.   This was agreed
to, and the air was filled with the song of the min-
strels and the music of trumpets, instead of the
discordant sounds of battle.

Peace on Earth.

(Recitation for a high-school pupil.)

The shepherds went their hasty way,
    And found the lowly stable shed
Where the Virgin-Mother lay ;
    And now they checked their eager tread,
For to the Babe that at her bosom clung
A mother's song the Virgin-Mother sung.

They told her how a glorious light,
    Streaming from a heavenly throng,
Around them shone suspending night,
    While, sweeter than a mother's song,
Blest angels heralded the Saviour's birth,
Glory to God on high and Peace on Earth.

She listened to the tale divine,
    And closer still the Babe she prest;
And while she cried, The Babe is mine !
    The milk rushed faster to her breast ;
Joy rose within her like a summer's morn ;
Peace, Peace on Earth ! the Prince of Peace is born

Thou Mother of the Prince of Peace,
    Poor, simple, and of low estate !
That strife should vanish, battle cease,
    O why should this thy soul elate ?
Sweet music's loudest note, the poet' story—
Didst thou ne'er love to hear of fame and glory ?

And is not War a youthful king,
    A stately hero clad in mail ?
Beneath his footsteps laurels spring ;
    Him Earth's majestic monarch's hail
Their friend, their playmate ! and his bold bright eye
Compels the maiden's love-confessing sigh.

"Tell this in some more courtly scene,
    To maids and youths in robes of state !

I am a woman poor and mean,
　And therefore is my soul elate.
War is a ruffian, all with guilt defiled,
That from the aged father tears his child !

" A murderous fiend, by fiends adored,
　He kills the sire and starves the son ;
The husband kills, and from her hoard
　Steals all his widow's toil had won ;
Plunders God's world of beauty ; rends away
All safety from the night, all comfort from the day.

" Then wisely is my soul elate,
　That strife should vanish, battle cease ;
I'm poor and of a low estate,
　The Mother of the Prince of Peace.
Joy rises in me like a summer's morn ;
Peace, Peace on Earth ! the Prince of Peace is born."
　　　　　　　　　　　　—S. T. Coleridge.

The Christmas Tree.

(Recitation for a boy to give before a Christmas tree is dismantled.)

Of all the trees in the woods and fields
　There's none like the Christmas tree ;
Tho' rich and rare is the fruit he yields,
　The strangest of trees is he.
Some drink their fill from the shower or rill ;
　No cooling draught needs he ;
Some bend and break when the storms awake,
　But they reach not the Christmas tree.
When wintry winds thro' the forests sweep,
　And snow robes the leafless limb ;
When cold and still is the ice-bound deep,
　O this is the time for him.
Beneath the dome of the sunny home,
　He stands with all his charms ;
'Mid laugh and song from the youthful throng,
　As they gaze on his fruitful arms.

There's golden fruit on the Christmas tree,
    And gems for the fair and gay ;
The lettered page for the mind bears he,
    And robes for the wintry day.
And there are toys for the girls and boys ;
    And eyes that years bedim
Grow strangely bright, with a youthful light,
    As they pluck from the pendant limb.

Old English Christmases.

The court celebrations of Christmas were observed with great splendor during the reign of King Charles the First. The royal family, with the lords and ladies, often took part themselves in the performances, and the cost to prepare costumes and sceneries for one occasion often amounted to ten thousand dollars. During Charles's reign, and preceding his, Ben Jonson wrote the plays, or masques, for Christmas. The court doings were, of course, copied outside by the people, and up to the twelfth night after Christmas, sports and feastings held high carnival.

So important were these Christmas court celebrations held by our ancestors, and of such moment were the preparations, that a special officer was appointed to take them in charge. To him were accorded large privileges, very considerable appointments, and a retinue equal to a prince's, counting in a chancellor, treasurer, comptroller, vice-chamberlain, divine, philosopher, astronomer, poet, physician, master of requests, clown, civilian, ushers, pages, footmen, messengers, jugglers, herald, orator, hunters, tumblers, friar, and fools. Over this mock court the mock monarch presided during the holidays with a reign as absolute as the actual monarch.

Holly and Ivy.

(Noël is the French word for Christmas.)

Holly standeth in ye house
  When that Noël draweth near;
Evermore at ye door
Standeth Ivy, shivering sore,
  In ye night wind bleak and drear.

"Sister Holly," Ivy quoth,
  "What is that within you see?
To and fro doth ye glow
Of ye yule-log flickering go;
  Would its warmth did cherish me!
Where thou bidest is it warm;
I am shaken of ye storm."

"Sister Ivy," Holly quoth,
  "Brightly burns the yule-log here,
And love brings beauteous things,
While a guardian angel sings
  To the babes that slumber near;
But, O Ivy! tell me now,
What without there seest thou?"

"Sister Holly," Ivy quoth,
  "With fair music comes ye Morn,
And afar burns ye Star
Where ye wondering shepherds are,
  And the Shepherd King is born:
'Peace on earth, good will to men,'
Angels cry, and cry again."

Holly standeth in ye house
  When that Noël draweth near;
Clambering o'er yonder door,
Ivy standeth evermore;
  And to them that rightly hear,
Each one speaketh of ye love
That outpoureth from Above.

—Eugene Field.

Holiday Chimes.

(When it is impossible to prepare a regular Christmas program for the friends of the pupils to enjoy with the school, the entrance to holiday week may be signalled by the impromptu reading and recitation of Christmas sentiments.)

CHRISTMAS DAY.

Feathery flakes are falling, falling
From the skies in softest way,
And between are voices calling,
"Soon it will be Christmas day!"
—*Mary B. Dodge.*

OLD DECEMBER.

With snowy locks December stands
'Mid sleet and storm; his wasted hands
A frosty scepter grasp and hold;
His frame is bent, his limbs are old;
His bearded lips are iced and pale;
He shivers in the winter gale.
Come then, O day of warm heart-cheer,
Make glad the waste and waning year,
While old December shivering goes
To rest beneath the drifted snows!
—*Benj. F. Leggett.*

CHRISTMAS-TIDE.

O happy chime,
O blessed time,
That draws us all so near!
"Welcome, dear day,"
All creatures say,
For Christmas-tide has come.
—*L. M. Alcott.*

CHRISTMAS EVE.

The time draws near the birth of Christ :
  The moon is hid ; the night is still ;
  The Christmas bells from hill to hill
Answer each other in the mist.

Rise, happy morn ! rise, holy morn !
  Draw forth the cheerful day from night :
  O Father ! touch the east, and light
The light that shone when hope was born.
—*Alfred Tennyson*

FATHER CHRISTMAS.

Here comes old Father Christmas,
  With sound of fife and drums,
With misteltoe about his brows,
  So merrily he comes !

Hurrah for Father Christmas !
  Ring all the merry bells !
And bring the grandsires all around
  To hear the tale he tells.
—*Rose Terry Cooke.*

CHRISTMAS IN ENGLAND.

Well our Christian sires of old
Loved when the year its course had rolled,
And brought blithe Christmas back again,
With all his hospitable train.
    *   *   *   *   *   *
England was merry England when
Old Christmas brought his sports again.
'Twas Christmas broached the mightiest ale ;
'Twas Christmas told the merriest tale,
A Christmas gambol oft could cheer
The poor man's heart through half the year.
—*Sir Walter Scott.*

MUSIC OF CHRISTMAS.

What do the angels sing ?
What is the word they bring ?
What is the music of Christmas again ?
  Glad tidings still to thee,
  Peace and good will to thee
Glory to God in the highest !
                    —*F. R. Havergal.*

A CHRISTMAS WISH.

A bright and blessed Christmas Day,
  With echoes of the angels' song,
And peace that cannot pass away,
  And holy gladness, calm and strong,
And sweetheart carols, flowing free !
This is my Christmas wish to thee.
                    —*F. R. Havergal.*

THE FIRST CHRISTMAS.

Where love takes, let love give, and so doubt not :
            Love counts but the will,
And the heart has its flowers of devotion
            No winter can chill ;
They who cared for " good will " that first Christmas
            Will care for it still.
                    —*A. A. Procter.*

ONCE A YEAR.

At Christmas play and make good cheer,
For Christmas comes but once a year.
                    —*Tusser.*

OLD ENGLISH SONG.

When Rosemary and Bays, the poet's crown,
Are bawled in frequent cries through all the town,

Then judge the festival of Christmas near,—
Christmas, the joyous period of the year !
Now with bright holly all the temples are strow ;
With Laurel green and sacred Mistletoe.

OLD FATHER CHRISTMAS.

Old Father Christmas is passing by,
His cheeks are ruddy, he's bright of eye ;
His beard is white with the snows of time.
His brow is hoary with frost and rime.
It's little he cares for the frost and the cold,
For old Father Christmas he never grows old.

EVERGREEN AND HOLLY.

Bring the evergreens and holly,
    Bring the music and the song,
Chase away the melancholy,
By the pleasures bright and jolly,
    Which to Christmas time belong.
                        —*E. O. Peck.*

How to Celebrate Arbor Day in the Schoolroom.

For the Primary, Grammar, and High School.

This book contains 96 solid pages. All the selections are fresh and new, and are selected both for their excellence and their practical usefulness in making up a program for the day. The following table of contents will give an idea of the book:

I THE ORIGIN OF ARBOR DAY.
II. HINTS ON PLANTING THE TREES.
III. ARBOR DAY IN THE U. S.
IV. SPECIAL EXERCISES.
1. The Arbor Day Queen; 2. Thoughts About Trees; 3. Little Runaways; 4. November's Party; 5. The Coming of Spring; 6. Through the Year with the Trees; 7. May; 8. The Poetry of Spring; 9. The Plea of the Trees; 10. Tree Planting Exercise.
V. RECITATIONS AND SONGS.
VI. FIFTY QUOTATIONS.
VII. THE PINK ROSE DRILL.
VIII. ARBOR DAY PROGRAMS
For Primary, Grammar, and High Schools.

Suggestions as to the most effective use of each exercise and recitation and the seven Arbor Day Programs are features which will be appreciated by the busy teacher.

Price, 25 Cents Postpaid.

How to Celebrate Washington's Birthday in the Schoolroom.

Containing Patriotic Exercises, Declamations, Recitations, Drills, Quotations, &c., for the
PRIMARY, GRAMMAR, AND HIGH SCHOOL.

96 Pages. Price, 25 Cents Postpaid.

This book has been received with great eagerness by teachers, and a large number sold. There are at least 100,000 teachers, who will hold some exercises on this great day. The observance of Washington's Birthday is increasing. It has recently been made compulsory in all the schools of New Jersey. No book is so good for preparing for it as this. The material is new and of a high order of merit. Here is a part of the

CONTENTS :

Special Exercises
His Birthday,
Tableaux and Recitations,
Our National Songs,
Historic Exercise,
Honoring the Flag,
Washington is Our Model,
Pictures from the Life of Washington,
Celebrating Washington's Birthday.

Recitations and Songs
The 22d of February,

I Would Tell,
Flag of the Rainbow,
The Good Old Days,
The School-House Stands by the Flag,
A Boy's Protest,
Tribute to Washington,
Our Presidents,
Flag of the Free.

Three Flag Drills

Fifty Patriotic Quotations.

Spring and Summer School Celebrations

EXERCISES, TABLEAUX, PANTOMIMES, RECITA-
TIONS, DRILLS, SONGS FOR CELEBRATING
EASTER, MAY DAY, MEMORIAL DAY,
FOURTH OF JULY, CLOSING DAY
IN THE SCHOOLROOM.

60 Pages. Price, 25 Cents Postpaid.

You have general exercises in your school, do you not? Then you need this book and should send for it now. It is illustrated. It contains nearly *one hundred* fresh, charming, mostly original selections.

PARTIAL TABLE OF CONTENTS:

Easter Song,	May and the Flowers,
Give Flowers to the Children,	The May Festival,
Easter in Early Days,	Gathering Flowers,
Sir Robin,	The Return of the Wanderers,
To the Flowers,	The Nation's Dead.
Wreath Drill and March,	In Memoriam,
Easter Time,	Zouave Drill,
Tableaux for Longfellow's King Robert	Program for Memorial Day,
of Sicily.	The Blue and the Gray,
A Bunch of Lilies.	The Nation's Birthday,
Greeting to May,	Stand by the Flag,
A Call to the Flowers,	Flag of Our Nation Great,
A Carpet of Green,	Boy's Marching Song,
To the Cuckoo,	The Poet's History of America,
To the Arbutus,	Etc., Etc.

Fancy Drills and Marches.

MOTION SONGS AND ACTION PIECES FOR ARBOR DAY,
CHRISTMAS DAY, MEMORIAL DAY, AND
PATRIOTIC OCCASIONS.

Price 25 Cents Postpaid.

THE LATEST, BRIGHTEST, AND BEST BOOK OF DRILLS.

Teachers who want something new and bright in the line of drills will certainly be greatly pleased with this book. One drill alone—Betz's Flag Grouping—has heretofore been sold for the price of this book, 25 cents.

PARTIAL TABLE OF CONTENTS:

Fancy Ribbon March. *Carl Betz.*	Wreath Drill and March.
Hatchet Drill for Feb. 22.	Rainbow Drill.
Christmas Tree Drill.	Glove Drill.
Wand Drill. *Mara L. Pratt.*	Tambourine Drill.
Delsarte Children. *M. D. Sterling.*	Flag Grouping and Posing. *Carl Betz.*
Zouave Drill.	Two Flag Drills.
Scarf Drill.	The March of the Red, White, and Blue.

Also many Motion Songs and Action Pieces. Full directions with each; fully illustrated,

BOOKS —BY— *T. G. ROOPER.*

These are the authorized editions, complete with topic
headings and other aids for the student and are
half the price of others.

APPERCEPTION:

OR "A POT OF GREEN FEATHERS," is a very simple book on psychology—strange as the title may seem. It discusses perception and shows
how perception becomes apperception. It is a book that any teacher may
read with profit. Commissioner Harris recommends it, so do other emi-
nent educators. Remember this edition has many special points of excellence. It is accurate, has paragraph headings, is clearly printed and
well bound in limp cloth.

Price 25c.; to teachers, 20c.; postage 3c.

OBJECT TEACHING:

OR WORDS AND THINGS. The author has done an important service
to teachers in pointing out thus clearly the foundation principles on which
the much-talked-of but little understood subject of Object Teaching should
be based.

It takes a simple subject—the Duck—and gives a very clear and correct
exposition of the right method of Object Teaching by a series of lessons.
The teacher will be set to work in the right direction by reading it. There
are plenty of books which furnish material for Object Lessons; no other
that gives so admirably the principles and method.

This edition is published by special permission of the author who has
written a preface and added topic headings and questions for the student.

**Limp cloth, 16mo. Price 25c.; to teachers, 20c.;
by mail, 3c. extra.**

STUDIES AND OCCUPATIONS.

Suitable for Children between the ages of 7 and 9. Everything that Mr.
Rooper writes is instructive and interesting. This is a practical and sug-
gestive discussion of what should be the child's work in school between the
ages of seven and nine, with a time table, or program based upon the
author's ideas. It is reprinted from the Summer Number (1894) of THE
SCHOOL JOURNAL. Only a limited edition has been issued and it will not
be reprinted.

Manilla Covers. Price, 15c. postpaid.

DRAWING IN INFANT SCHOOLS:

A STUDY IN PRACTICAL PSYCHOLOGY. All of Mr. Rooper's writings on
educational topics are based upon careful observation and experiment, and
are extremely practical and interesting. This little book is no exception.
Everyone interested in the study of the mental development of the child
should read it.

Manilla Covers. Price, 15c. postpaid.

The First Three Years of Childhood.

An exhaustive study of the psychology of children. By
BERNARD PEREZ. Edited and translated by Alice M.
Christie, translator of "Child and Child Nature," with
an introduction by James Sully, M. A., author of "Out-
lines of Psychology," etc. 12mo, cloth, 340 pp. Price,
$1.50 ; *to teachers,* $1.20 ; by mail, 10 cts. extra.

This is a comprehensive treatise on the psychology of childhood, and is a practical study of the human mind, not full
formed and equipped with knowledge, but as nearly as
possible, *ab origine*—before habit, environment, and education have asserted their sway and made their permanent
modifications. The writer looks into all the phases of child
activity. He treats exhaustively, and in bright Gallic style,
of sensations, instincts, sentiments, intellectual tendencies,
the will, the faculties of æsthetic and moral senses of young
children. He shows how ideas of truth and falsehood arise
in little minds, how natural is imitation and how deep is
credulity. He illustrates the development of imagination and
the elaboration of new concepts through judgment, abstrac-
tion, reasoning, and other mental methods. It is a book that
has been long wanted by all who are engaged in teaching,
and especially by all who have to do with the education and
training of children.

Our edition has a new index of special value and is beauti-
fully printed and elegantly and durably bound.

Prof. John Fiske, Harvard University: "It seems to me an excellent book and very much needed."

John Bascom, President University of Wisconsin: "A work of
marked interest to psychologists and intelligent parents."

B. A. Hinsdale, ex-Supt. Schools, Cleveland, Ohio: "I have exam-
ined the book with much pleasure and profit, and I sincerely hope you
may be successful in introducing it generally among the teachers of the
country."

Edwin C. Hewitt, President Illinois State Normal University:
"You have rendered an excellent service in bringing the book before
the public. I hope both your house and the public will profit by a
large sale."

**G. Stanley Hall, Professor of Psychology and Pedagogy, Johns
Hopkins University:** "I esteem the work a very valuable one for
primary and kindergarten teachers and for all interested in the psychology of childhood."

**Col. Francis W. Parker, Principal Cook County Normal and
Training School, Chicago:** "I am glad to see that you have published
Perez's wonderful work upon childhood. I shall do all I can to get
everybody to read it. It is a grand work."

www.ingramcontent.com/pod-product-compliance
Lightning Source LLC
Chambersburg PA
CBHW020026030726
47499CB00007B/2293